FORGIVE THE MESSENGER

ANTONIO MARTELLO

ISBN 13: 9780999347805
ISBN 10: 0999347802

www.forgivethemessenger.com

Facebook: https://www.facebook.com/groups/889752791178926/

Twitter: @AMartelloBooks

For my sister, Roxann

CONTENTS

1. MIDNIGHT'S WARNING   7
2. FROM DESPAIR, HOPE ARISES   9
3. PRAYERS ANSWERED?   11
4. AN OLD NIGHTMARE PLAYS AGAIN   17
5. ENLISTING HELP TO KEEP THE DOOR CLOSED   19
6. JOEL STANDS FIRM   21
7. JOEL MEETS JOHNNY   25
8. GETTING SPUN IN RASHID'S WEB   29
9. THEN THE DOOR WILL NOT STAY CLOSED   35
10. JOHNNY HELPS JOEL OUT   41
11. JOEL SAYS GOODBYE TO A JOB WELL DONE   43
12. JOHNNY LEARNS THE TRUTH ABOUT REGGIE   45
13. FIRST STRIKE   49
14. FAMILY BONDING   53
15. PAUL CONFRONTS EVIL   57
16. WHO IS PAUL?   61
17. PAUL MEETS PHILOMENA   65
18. THE DEVIL'S WORM   69
19. A STARTLING VISION   73
20. NO LONGER PART OF THE FAMILY   75
21. TOMAS'S OFFER   77
22. ASSASSINS' REMORSE   81
23. A SHOCKING CONFESSION   87
24. THE NEW MOVEMENT   95
25. AN UNFORTUNATE INCIDENT   101
26. UNEXPECTED VISITORS   105
27. JOHNNY MEETS THE SUPERIOR GENERAL'S "CREW"   107
28. JOHNNY PUTS OFF TOMAS—AGAIN   111
29. CAUGHT ON CAMERA?   113
30. RASHID HATCHES A PLAN   115
31. PRAYERS ANSWERED   119
32. THE FACE OF THE ENEMY   121

33. A New Life   125
34. Are Two Pauls Better Than One?   127
35. Vito's Ultimatum   129
36. A Desperate Plan   131
37. Johnny Deepens His Obligation   135
38. Race for the Border   137
39. Troubling News   141
40. Pearls Before Swine   143
41. Wolves at Their Door   147
42. On the Road Again   151
43. Not Quite Tourists   155
44. A Battle in Quebec   159
45. Home Sweet Rome   163
46. The Rise of the Beast   167
47. The Return of Arturo   171
48. The Clock Strikes Twelve   175
49. Mikey, "Hot Dog," the Angel   177
50. Deep Questions   181
51. The Beginning of the End   183
52. Revelation   185
53. Meeting with the Ayatollah   191
54. Clouds of Doom   195
55. On the Razor's Edge   199
56. Never Add Insult to Injury   203
57. The Unlucky, Lucky One   207
58. The Lord Works in Strange Ways   211

Acknowledgments   213
About the Author   215

1

MIDNIGHT'S WARNING

Elmira State Prison, New York

"I'm going to take that old white motherfucker's stuff," says Flakes, a tall, lean black inmate, his nickname coming from the breakfast cereal he eats every morning.

"That's no old man, cuz," his friend, Midnight, whispers as the two of them stand outside an open cell, where a white man is sleeping while standing up, his back to them. Midnight is a short, stocky, muscular man who received his nickname from the police due to his midnight burglaries.

"That's Johnny Greaseball Dynamite. He will inflict serious harm on you. For real, son."

"Nah, Fuck that shit!" Flakes says. "He's got some serious cartons of cigarettes in there. Let's do this."

Midnight shakes his head. "Flakes, it's not what you think. He caught two bodies. He is one insane man. Please, don't do this! If you do, you'll be doing it on your own."

Midnight walks away, crossing and uncrossing his arms, signaling he wants no part of it. Flakes seizes the moment to slip into Johnny's cell.

An inner alarm goes off in Johnny. One eye shoots open, and he looks at a piece of broken mirror placed strategically on his cell wall. His reaction is quick, deliberate, and deadly. He strikes once with precision and accuracy, plunging a sharp makeshift knife, made from a sharpened metal bed railing, into his intruder's neck, severing a main artery.

Flakes staggers out of the cell, gasping for air and pointing to his throat, which has a gaping six-inch slit with blood gushing from it. He looks around desperately for someone to help, but help cannot come soon enough. His legs give way, and he collapses to the concrete floor. He gazes helplessly into the heavens as he loses his struggle for life and accepts death's calling. Life's energy leaves him, causing his reaching arms to fall. Soon, the only motion coming from him is his blood, which pumps out of his body, forming a dark red pool around him.

2

FROM DESPAIR, HOPE ARISES

Johnny's daughter, Reginella, affectionately called Reggie, walks barefoot down the street in an old Italian Bronx neighborhood often referred to as Little Italy or Arthur Avenue, popular for its food shops and restaurants. As she walks, her feet get cut and scraped from sharp objects. Either she doesn't notice, or she doesn't care. Older Italian women who are shopping have known the young girl since birth and call to her, but she is oblivious to their voices as she staggers through the streets in a heroin-hazed high. One of the women scrambles to summon her friend, the young girl's grandmother, Johnny's mother, Philomena.

When they reach her home, she is caring for her granddaughter's baby, an interracial child, half-white and half-black. The baby's daddy is not only her granddaughter's boyfriend; he is also her pimp and her heroin provider. He beats her brutally to keep her turning tricks for him.

The old woman relieves Philomena of the baby, and Philomena runs as fast as she can, wearing her house dress, which is her preferred style of dress these days. Her seventy-five years of age cannot be denied, but her face is still pretty, and her grandmotherly looks suit her in her golden years. She puts her salt-and-pepper hair up in a bun and finds a pair of Reggie's shoes. Then she heads toward the area her granddaughter was spotted.

By the time she gets there, Reggie's captor has brought her back to his ghetto apartment to resume turning tricks for him. Philomena races to his front courtyard. "Reginella! Reggie!" she cries, tears flowing from her eyes. "I have your shoes!" she says, holding them up. Her lips quiver, and her body shakes with inner pain. Rashid, Reggie's pimp, looks out his courtyard window and then dumps a bucket of water on Philomena, soaking her.

She leaves and then returns with an umbrella, calling again, "*Reginella, ti amo così tanto. Ti prego di tornare a casa, ti prego di tornare a casa,*" ("Reginella, I love you so much. Please come home, please come home,") while johns walk past her on the way to have their way with her grand-daughter. When there is no response, she leaves in helpless anguish.

She gathers herself and walks to Mount Carmel Church, dazed and confused. She drops to her knees before the statue of the Blessed Mother. Sobbing and holding her head in her hands, she shakes her head and yells at the statue through her tears. "Why, why? When I did all the things I was supposed to do on this earth to receive your love . . . why is this happening to me?" Sobbing uncontrollably, Philomena is on the brink of collapse, her feeling of inner peace and solitude, her belief in the Church's teachings and promises that being compliant would grant her a peaceful and fulfilling life, the holy understanding between her and her God has been shattered.

"What did I do wrong?" she sobs. "Why have you left me?"

On the brink of passing out from the emotional pain, she feels a tap on her clasped hands. Wanting to be left alone, she ignores it. She remains on her knees, her eyes closed. More tapping. She slowly opens her eyes and lifts her head to see who is touching her. She peers around, but no one is there. The church is empty.

She looks at her hands and notices drops of blood. The blood has the pleasing scent of roses. It fills her senses, calming her. Tilting her head up, she looks at the statue and sees blood tears streaming from Mary's eyes, running down her face, and falling from the precise spot needed to hit her hands. Philomena is shocked, but she remains outwardly calm. Inside, her thoughts race, overwhelming her brain. *Is Mother Mary crying with me? Has she heard my prayers? Will she answer them?*

Thinking this is a sign from the Blessed Mother, she grabs tissues from her purse and dabs up the blood from the statue, thanking Mary. Then she stuffs the blood-soaked tissues into her purse and hurries home, certain her prayers have been heard. Surely, it is a sign from God.

Her despair gone, she feels a new sense of energy that she has not known for many years. Her feelings of anguish and helplessness have been erased. New hope springs eternal in Philomena Ciminetti.

3

PRAYERS ANSWERED?

The next morning, Philomena's doorbell rings. When she opens the door, she is met by a portly, young Jewish man wearing a yarmulke.

"Is Philomena here?" he asks.

"Yes, that's me," she says, though puzzled by his appearance.

He stands a little straighter. "Hi. My name is Joel Rosenbaum. A friend at Fordham University told me you were renting an apartment."

"Yes, I am, but I've never rented to a Jewish person before. I only cook Italian."

Her light Italian accent makes the law student smile. "Well, Philomena, I have relatives in Rome, so this will not be the first time Jews have lived amongst Italians."

She smiles politely. "Okay, if it's not a problem for you. But why are you renting now in the middle of a semester?"

A tired expression overtakes his face. "The young students are making so much noise, I can't get any sleep."

Philomena frowns. "Aren't you a little old for college? You look to be about thirty-five."

Joel smiles at her question. "I'm thirty-six, and I'm a lawyer by day and a student by night. I have an upcoming trial concerning canon law. So, I'm taking classes to familiarize myself.

Philomena nods, satisfied with his answer. "Okay, come in," she says, welcoming him into her quaint two-family home. Joel enters a clean, well-kept hallway with darkly stained cherry wood railings and wainscoting throughout the hallway and up the stairs. The steps are rugged, and brightly colored floral wallpaper adorns the walls. Dimly lit wall sconces illuminate the hallway. He notices an open door on the left side of the first floor that leads into Philomena's apartment. Philomena leads him up the stairs to the three-room apartment that she is offering for

11

rent. Once she reaches the landing in front of the apartment's door, she stops and turns to him. She continues, "There's no better place to take that kind of course than Fordham University, a Jesuit college."

Philomena takes him on a guided tour of her warm and welcoming fully furnished three-room apartment. All the rooms are nicely sized, consisting of a kitchen, living room, and a full bathroom with a shower head attached to a pipe that sticks out of a wall aimed into a original antique tub with a fully functional old pull-chain toilet. The bedroom has a dark wooden dresser matching the dark solid oak-framed bed that has freshly laid laundered sheets. It is all so quiet, cozy, and inviting to Joel. He accepts the terms and the rental amount, giving her two months' rent in advance.

"Can I get some sleep now?" he asks. "I have night classes tonight, and I did not sleep well last night. Would you mind?"

"But you have no luggage," Philomena replies, dumbfounded.

He smiles. "I will bring it tomorrow."

Still confused, Philomena shrugs. "Go ahead, I guess." She leaves, closing the door behind her. *He seems harmless enough. Could this be God's answer to my prayer?* she wonders. *I would think God would send a strong warrior type. This can't be anything more than another renter from the college.* She's had many renters throughout the years to supplement her income.

The next morning, Philomena is at the bottom of the stairs waiting for her new tenant to walk down. When he emerges from his apartment, shuffling down the stairs, she asks. "Would you like coffee or something to eat?"

He smiles sadly. "No, sorry, I only eat kosher food, but thank you anyway."

By mid-afternoon, with her great-granddaughter in tow, Philomena takes three buses to Riverdale, a section in the Bronx that is heavily populated with Jewish residents. She finds a kosher butcher and grocery store and speaks to the resident rabbi at the butcher shop. He gives her instructions on how to cook a kosher meal. He says his instructions must be followed exactly for it to be a truly kosher meal. Philomena buys dishes and pots that need to be kept separate and gathers everything else that's required. It is all that she and her great-granddaughter can hold. Then they board the bus for home.

At 6 p.m., Joel arrives at his newly rented apartment. Familiar smells of kosher meats and spices with a twist of Italian flavoring fill his senses, igniting a hunger in his stomach. As he looks down at the front door, he sees shopping bags from a kosher Jewish butcher and grocery store, even pots and dishware covers from a well-known kosher manufacturer. He can hardly control his excitement and surprise. Then he stops and thinks for a moment. *Why would this woman show so much kindness to a stranger?* He is overwhelmed by her warmth and the extra effort from one human being, who has so little, to another.

The door to Philomena's apartment cracks open, and she looks out at Joel. "What are you waiting for? Sit down! Time to *mangia* (eat)!"

Joel can hardly get to the table fast enough to enjoy an Italian-kosher meal for the first time in his life. Pasta dishes made with kosher noodles, Italian sauces with all-kosher ingredients, and meatballs made from kosher beef. She even found a kosher wine in a hidden-away wine store in Riverdale.

As he enjoys the meal, he can't help but notice a small interracial child asleep on the couch in the living room. He slugs down a gullet-clearing swallow of wine. Savoring the taste of a kaleidoscope of herbs and spices causes a "spice high," a sensation-filling sense of taste like no other culinary experience he has had before.

He wipes his lips, rolls his eyes back, and nods, pointing at the food and flashing the "okay" sign several times as he clears his throat. "Without question, this was one of the most delightful, wonderful, and amazing meals I've ever had the pleasure of eating. I've never had kosher-Italian. This is something to write home about."

Philomena bows her head and smiles in acknowledgment. "Thank you. It makes cooking worth it to see someone enjoy the food so much. Please, enjoy!"

Joel smiles. "I am! I mean, I did! And its memories will last a lifetime." Joel's eyes have taken on a glassy glow due to the kosher wine. He nods toward her living room. "Are you babysitting?"

"No, that is my granddaughter's baby."

He squints to comprehend what his ears have just ingested. The child's complexion and features are more African than white. "Oh, very cute child. Where is your granddaughter?"

Tears start to roll down the old woman's face. He sits up straight in his chair, alarmed at Philomena's reaction. "I'm sorry if I caused you any sad thoughts." He puts his hand on her shoulder to console her.

She wipes away her tears. "No, it's nothing you said. It is something I will always have to live with now. The events that have shaped my life in my last years."

"If you feel like talking, I'm a great listener," he says. "Besides, I still have half a bottle of wine. Please go on; it may make you feel better."

She is reluctant, but Joel comforts her as he dips his challah bread into her kosher tomato sauce, smiles, and then shoves it into his mouth. He nods softly smiling, coaxing her to speak.

Joel's warm personality wears her down, and she tells him about her beloved son, Johnny, who was all she had left after her husband passed. She explains how he ran with a rough crowd, got himself in trouble, and was sent to prison for the rest of his life.

"Johnny's wife left, abandoned her daughter, and she doesn't even call. I wasn't paying enough attention to my granddaughter, and she met a drug dealer on the computer. He lives in the area. He got her hooked on drugs and got her pregnant. Now the baby is mine to take care of, and I can't let the baby go. She's my blood. I'm so attached to her. I love her, and she will be with me until I die. I never thought at my age I would have to raise my granddaughter's baby from birth."

Joel is saddened by the heartbreaking story she tells in her Italian accent, but he is mesmerized as she goes on to recount Johnny's trial and how his lawyer threw his case.

Philomena does not know it, but she is talking to one of the greatest legal minds in the world. He practices law in ten countries and speaks as many languages fluently. He comes from a wealthy and influential Jewish family, who have earned their wealth through European banking for the past two hundred years. His family's philanthropy is legendary throughout the world, especially within Jewish circles. Their wealth is in the hundreds of billions of dollars.

How did Joel wind up in Philomena's apartment? Perhaps through divine intervention, or perhaps because Joel is taking night classes at Fordham University to learn about canon law. It may also be due to Joel's desire to feel close to whatever community he is residing in by living amongst the locals, making his experience as true to life as possible. Maybe a bit of all. Whatever the reason, Joel is there.

Joel is one of God's "chosen," someone who is blessed and gifted by God. With a sharp, quick, deep-thinking, analytical brain, he is a genius, on par with Einstein, one of the world's elite legal minds. Law is his passion, and a tough case rejected by others is his top priority. He takes cases for no fee when no one else will. He shuns the spotlight and keeps a low profile. Money is neither important nor rewarding to him. His family loves and supports him and his causes. Have Philomena's prayers at the Mount Carmel Church been answered in the person of Joel Rosenbaum?

Joel is intrigued by the woman's woes. He asks if she has any of Johnny's court files and documents; he would like to look at them. She says she has everything and will leave them outside his apartment later. Joel thanks her for a great dinner and then heads up to his room.

The next day, showered and ready to start on his way to the university, Joel opens his apartment door and finds a pile of file boxes that Philomena brought up during the night. Joel chuckles slightly as he heads off to the university.

The next morning, the old woman comes home from shopping and finds two copies of a legal motion in front of her apartment door. They are thick and professionally done from front to back. She wonders how Joel could have read all those boxes of files and completed a motion so quickly. He could not possibly have read and comprehended all that and then produced a complete legal motion in just one day. After many years of having lawyers produce motion after motion, it has always taken at least two to three months.

She walks up the stairs and sees all the boxes moved around and stacked neatly in a different order than she had left them, with new tags and new stickers on them. Little does she realize that Joel just needs to glance at a paper for his mind to absorb its contents. Then it is embedded in his mind, always available for recall. It works much faster than a photographic memory.

Philomena is ecstatic, thinking that maybe Joel's motion can free Johnny, and when Johnny comes back, he will make everything right. She will have her family back and be whole again, able to die in peace.

When Joel returns from his classes, Philomena meets him at the door, vibrant and full of positive energy. He smells food, only this time there are many different aromas, and when he peeks inside, he sees enough food for a banquet. He looks back at her, barely suppressing a grin. "I assume you've seen the motion?"

She smiles. "Yes, and I have read it through. It seems like there is real reason for hope. My nephew is a law student, and he thinks it is a real winner."

Joel laughs. "Smart boy, your nephew! But there is no guarantee it will get Johnny out. The way I see it, Johnny has two important legal issues on his side to win. I will stop by the courts and file the motions tomorrow."

Philomena's friends and family start to arrive. Her girlfriends, her brother, and her nephew all congratulate Joel. He smiles, thankful for their encouragement, but he warns them the case is far from over. It still must go through the courts.

Joel is basing his motion on the fact that, in one of the killings for which Johnny was convicted, there was prosecutorial misconduct. The prosecutor told Johnny to admit the gun found at the scene was his, even though it was not found on him, and they would not charge him with the murder; he could walk out of there. So, Johnny admitted the gun was his.

"You have just incriminated yourself," the prosecutor said. "The bullets from your gun match the bullet inside the victim."

Second, if he is let off the first murder, Johnny has already served enough time for the second murder for which he was convicted. They will have to let him come home.

4

AN OLD NIGHTMARE PLAYS AGAIN

Two months later, at 10 a.m., at the Bronx district attorney's office at 161st Street and the Grand Concourse, a young secretary summons her boss, District Attorney Calvin Jones, the first African American man to hold that office. She informs him that Judge Sol Klein, from the New York State Supreme Court Appellate Division, is calling.

Calvin picks up the phone. "Yes, Judge?"

"Hello, Calvin," a distinguished-sounding voice replies. "Do you remember the John Ciminetti case?"

Alarm bells go off in Calvin's head. "Of course, I prosecuted it before I was elected DA."

"Well, we believe he has a strong possibility of getting out, based on his new motion, and your office's reply to his motion is weak."

Calvin sinks in his chair. "Judge, you know how hard this office has worked to convict him and keep him in jail. He was a one-man crime wave. He needs to be kept off the streets."

"We can no longer sweep it under the rug," Judge Klein replies. "Powerful forces are behind this. We cannot get rid of it. Every time we try to dispose of it, it reappears. We're going to have to hear the motion and, as it stands, grant it."

Calvin sits there, stunned, as he thinks back to the mid-1980s, when he was a young DA working his way up as a prosecutor. Johnny Ciminetti was the case that helped cement his reputation. It was his crown jewel.

"Who's the lawyer on his motion?" he asks.

"Joel Rosenbaum."

"The philanthropist?"

17

"The same guy."

"What's wrong with him?" Calvin asks. "Has he any idea who he's helping?"

"I've got to go, Calvin. Just giving you a heads-up."

"Thanks, Judge."

As soon as he hangs up, Calvin summons his head investigators to his office. "I want to know everything about Joel Rosenbaum, the legal philanthropist. Get me his rabbi's name, phone number, and address. And I want to meet with his rabbi personally."

5

ENLISTING HELP TO KEEP THE DOOR CLOSED

At 9 a.m. the next morning, Calvin, along with Detective Mario "Bulldog" Mafucci, sit in the waiting room of the large synagogue in Manhattan, where Joel's family worships while in New York. Mafucci resembles his nickname—short, pudgy, and solid with a rounded face and a receding hairline. He is stubborn, unwilling to relent.

Rabbi Mordecai Spitz is a trusted friend and confidante to the Rosenbaum family. As his office door opens, his secretary, sitting behind her desk, speaks in an elevated voice. "Rabbi, the district attorney and a detective are here."

He nods and smiles, acknowledging their presence. "Please, come in. Would you like something to drink? Some strudel? Bagels? They're very good. We get them from Second Avenue."

Calvin smiles. "No, thank you."

Rabbi Spitz waves them into his office. "Please, come in, sit." He motions to two chairs in front of his desk.

Rabbi Spitz sits in his chair behind his desk, stroking his beard, a perplexed look on his face. "What is so urgent that you needed to see me on such short notice?"

"Rabbi, one of your members is doing something we feel is wrong and is going to lead to a lot of trouble," Calvin begins, speaking in a respectful tone.

"What is he doing?" Rabbi Spitz asks, leaning forward.

"He's going to get a psychopath killer out of jail, allowing him to kill again," Bulldog says. "Are you familiar with a guy named John Ciminetti?"

The rabbi nods. "Yes, I heard about him in the eighties. I followed the

19

news coverage. I remember him well."

"Rabbi, we need to keep him in jail, so he can't hurt anyone ever again," Calvin says.

"Well . . . yes . . . I would hope so," the rabbi says, still not sure where this is going. "I am not in your business. How can I possibly help?"

Calvin looks at Mafucci and then back at Rabbi Spitz. "Will you speak to your member? Tell him to leave this man where he belongs and not help him anymore."

The rabbi puckers his lips. "Gentlemen, who are we talking about? Which member of my synagogue?"

"Joel Rosenbaum, the lawyer," Mafucci says.

The rabbi's thoughts go immediately to the large plaque on the outside of his building. This synagogue was funded by the kindness and generosity of the Rosenbaum family. Stunned, Rabbi Spitz remains silent as Calvin and Detective Mafucci continue speaking.

Realizing the rabbi is not interested in speaking any longer, Calvin and Mafucci stand up to leave. Calvin leaves a piece of paper on the rabbi's desk with the address and phone number of where Joel is staying in the Bronx. "Thank you for seeing us, Rabbi. If there is any assistance you can give us, it would be greatly appreciated."

"Yes, anytime," Rabbi Spitz replies, still in a daze.

Outside the rabbi's office, Bulldog turns to Calvin. "Did you see how he clammed up when we said it was Rosenbaum?"

Calvin nods, deep in thought. "I did, but I believe he will have a conversation with Rosenbaum. We'll have to wait and see what effect our visit has."

6

Joel Stands Firm

Joel has just finished getting dressed when he hears his doorbell ring. He hurries downstairs to the front door and is shocked to see Rabbi Spitz on his doorstep. "Rabbi, did something happen? Is it my mother or father?"

The rabbi shakes his head. "No, nothing like that, thank God."

"How did you find me?" Joel murmurs, still confused. "Were you just in the area?"

Rabbi Spitz looks at Joel with a concerned smile. "The district attorney from the Bronx, along with a homicide detective, came to see me at the synagogue."

"For what reason?"

The rabbi opens his hands in a gesture of prayer. "Over the Ciminetti case you're working on."

Joel squints. "That's odd. What did they say?"

"They would like for you to stop working on the case. They say the man is a homicidal maniac, and if you don't stop, you will be putting a killer back on the street."

Joel chuckles. "So, my motion is going to make it after all."

"Joel," the rabbi says, his voice taking on a serious tone, "to have a DA and a detective come to ask for my help is alarming."

"They didn't play fair," Joel replies. "They broke the rules to win their case."

"Joel, sometimes rules don't apply, such as when someone is on a killing spree."

Joel crosses his arms. "This case isn't just about Ciminetti. Think of the innocent people who these tactics will be used against just so someone can win a case. They're breaking the rules, and it has to be made right, or innocent people will be convicted. If so, what's the sense of having laws? What happened when Jews all over Europe were being slaughtered? There was a total disregard for the law. No, I will not leave this alone."

The rabbi shakes his head slowly. "Joel, leave this alone. It can only lead to more trouble."

"I'm sorry, Rabbi, but I have to do what is right."

Rabbi Spitz looks at his shoes for a moment and then raises his eyes and fixes them on Joel. "Do you ever have nightmares about bad people?"

"Yes, but—"

"Well, prison, not the streets, is where those nightmares must stay. You should not use your skills and your gifted mind to set one of those nightmares free."

"I'm sorry, Rabbi, but I must go forward."

The rabbi nods slowly, sensing Joel's conviction. "I see we are at an impasse. I am going to have to confer with your father. I will call Zurich tonight and seek his guidance on this matter."

Joel stares at Rabbi Spitz, realizing he will do everything in his power to prevent Joel from moving forward. "Rabbi, I will take some time to reflect about this. I will give you my answer tomorrow."

The rabbi nods in approval. "You're a good man, Joel. Detach yourself from this emotional crusade. Take a step back, and take a deep breath. I am sure you will come to the right conclusion when you take time to reflect and look at it from outside the box. I am sure you will come away with a different perspective. And Joel, I am sure your father has much more important things to do than to be bothered with a phone call from me. I will wait to hear from you."

As soon as the rabbi is gone, Joel's thoughts go immediately to Philomena. How is he going to tell her he is unable to continue? Feeling extremely down and upset, Joel decides to go for a walk.

Walking along 187th Street and the corner of Cambrelling Avenue, he sees Philomena walking, so he follows a block behind to see where she is going. When she hits the corner of Crotona Avenue, she makes a right turn. As she continues down the avenue, the area looks dangerous, and Joel becomes alarmed for her safety, as well as his.

After a brisk walk, she stops in the middle of a long block and walks into the courtyard between two buildings. "Reggie, I can't sleep," she says. "Come home; your daughter misses you. You need to come home."

On the left side of the courtyard, one of the doors to the building flies open, and Reggie, looking tired but still very attractive, appears. She runs to Philomena and embraces her, wiping away her tears.

"Grandma, it's not safe for you to be here."

Philomena kisses her. "Come home! You don't need to stay here. You belong home with your daughter and me. Your dad will be coming home soon. He won't like this."

"Grandma, I can't leave here. Rashid will hurt me, you, and the baby."

"No, he won't," Philomena says, fighting back tears. "Please, come home."

Reggie hugs and kisses her grandmother. "You better go. He'll be back soon."

Philomena, not yet willing to let go, holds her granddaughter tight.

Joel notices a tall mean-looking rapper-type gangster enter the courtyard. When Reggie sees him, she is gripped with fear. "Don't hurt her!" she says, shielding Philomena with her body. "It's not her fault! I came down to see her!"

Sensing Philomena is in trouble, Joel crosses the street and stands at the entrance to the courtyard. "Philomena, come away from there."

Rashid drops his groceries and smashes Reggie on the side of her face. Philomena grabs at him, and, in the tussle, he knocks her to the ground, grinding her face into the cement.

Joel enters the courtyard to help, and Rashid turns his attention to him. "Jew boy, you brought this old bitch here? Ha, motherfucker!"

Joel kneels down, trying to help Philomena, when he receives a vicious kick to the face. A flash of light fills his head.

As he slips into semi-consciousness, his mind flashes to an episode of *The X Factor*. One of the hosts yells from behind the curtain, in a heavy Scottish accent, as Susan Boyle sings, "You didn't expect that now, did you?"

He snaps out of it. He's dizzy and feels warm blood flowing from both nostrils as he staggers, still holding onto Philomena as he lifts her. He gets up, waving his attacker off. "Enough!" Then he staggers away with Philomena, both of them dazed and bloodied.

"Don't come back here, Jew boy, and keep that greaseball bitch away from here. If she comes back, I'll be looking for you. Fucking Jew motherfucker!"

Joel walks Philomena back to her house. She tells him how sorry she is he got hurt. He shouldn't have been there. It's all her fault.

Back in the apartment, Philomena presses cold compresses to the bridge of Joel's nose and the back of his neck, bringing the bleeding to a stop.

"What was that all about?" Joel asks, his head finally beginning to clear.

Philomena looks at him. The side of her face and her nose are scraped, and her eye is swollen. "That is my granddaughter, and that is her drug-dealer pimp. He keeps her high on drugs and makes her do whatever he wants."

"Why don't you go to the police?"

Philomena looks in the mirror and wipes her face. "They say they can't do anything. She's there of her own free will. She's scared of him and what he might do to the baby and to me if she leaves. He threatens her, says he'll kill me if she ever leaves."

Joel feels a deep hatred for his attacker. He makes sure Philomena is okay before he retires to his apartment.

He flicks on the light in his bathroom and stares in the mirror. Joel is filled with rage, unusual for someone who is not a violent man, but he wants revenge. His heart also breaks for the old woman. Does she really believe that if her son, Johnny, gets out he will be able to make things okay again? Maybe she's right—if Joel does his part. All he has to do is appear in front of the judge hearing Johnny's appeal, and Johnny will come home. He decides he wants to meet with Johnny.

The next morning, he asks Philomena to arrange it. She agrees, under the condition that Joel doesn't mention that Johnny has a granddaughter or tell her of Reggie's situation. "I'm not sure how he will handle it."

Joel agrees to her conditions, even though he thinks it's not the greatest idea, but who is he to interfere?

7

Joel Meets Johnny

It is a clear day, but it is unusually cool and crisp for a summer morning. Joel blows warm air into his hands as he waits to get inside the prison waiting room.

The guards ask Joel to empty his pockets into a basket on the table. Then they direct him through a metal detector and wave a metal wand over his body. After they clear him, they lead him into a waiting room for client/lawyer meetings. He is finally going to meet the man who has stirred so many conflicting emotions in him in such a short period of time in so many ways without ever meeting him.

Joel turns to the two guards standing in the room. "Are you going to be here throughout my visit?"

"It's for your own safety and that of the prison," one of the guards says. "If he tries to use you as a hostage to escape, it will cause a lot of trouble for us. However, you can request us to leave for the sake of lawyer/client privacy, and we will have to leave. It's your call."

Joel's mind races. Is all they say about Johnny true? Is he a sick psychopath, or have the guards been planted by the DA to listen to his strategy for the case?

"I would like our privacy, one on one," he says finally.

"Are you sure?" the guard asks.

"Yes, I am," Joel says, his tone defiant.

The sound of automatic jail doors opening, accompanied by voices and footsteps, gets closer.

"Okay, take the cuffs off," a guard says. Joel hears the clang of metal chains hitting the floor, followed by a key being placed into the thick metal door that leads into the visiting room.

The door opens, revealing a man in a prison-issued orange jumpsuit. He offers Joel a welcoming smile. Johnny's fine facial features blend nicely with his olive skin. His deep, dark, piercing eyes seem to draw Joel in to a deep vastness, a true killer's stare. He is a handsome man. His body is chiseled, his hair crew cut, almost shaved bald, and his stubbly beard has a touch of gray.

One of the guards looks at Joel. "Are you sure?"

Joel replies with a brief nod, and the guards go out.

The room is silent as Johnny settles into his seat. "How was the trip up?" he asks with a friendly grin.

"It was a nice drive," Joel replies cordially. "Some great scenery."

Johnny smiles. "My mom has told me some very nice things about you, Joel. And from what I hear and read about you, you're for the underdog and the innocent. I find it hard to understand. What's your interest in my case?"

Joel returns Johnny's smile. "Your mom's kosher-Italian cooking."

Both men laugh.

"Mom sure can cook!" Johnny says. "If you don't look out, your waistline will start to grow."

Joel pats his stomach, feeling the tension in the room begin to release. "It already has. She's a good old-fashioned woman. Her family is everything to her."

Johnny nods silently, his eyes on the table. Joel assumes he is thinking about his mother and daughter. Finally, Johnny looks up. "Yes, that she is. A really good woman. Hard to find these days."

Joel senses nothing of the viciousness he was warned about, no sign of lunacy or a disconnect with reality. *What am I missing here?* he wonders. *Come on, you're better than this. Am I being taken in by a master manipulator or a con man?* Despite his initial fears, he finds himself drawn to Johnny.

"Where did you get your face so banged up?" Johnny asks. Joel pushes his glasses up. "I, uh, I was reaching for a book. The shelf gave way and hit me."

Johnny tilts his head and smiles skeptically. "That shelf must have had an expensive pair of sneakers on it."

Joel puts his hand to his cheek, where the impression of sneaker laces is clearly visible.

"We see a lot of that in here," Johnny explains.

Johnny's keen eye astonishes Joel. "Well, let's leave that for now and talk about your case."

Their meeting lasts several hours. Johnny's comprehension of Joel's motion astonishes the young lawyer. His full understanding of the law is no easy task for a layman. If Johnny would have gone another way in life, he would have been a great lawyer.

"What will you do if you get out?" Joel asks.

Johnny shakes his head with regret. "I won't be so stupid this time."

"Do you mean not so stupid as to get caught for murder?"

"It's like this, Joel: I've lost so much and gained nothing. My life stopped twenty-four years ago. I have to make up for what I've lost. At my age, I'm fighting time. I need reconciliation with my family to heal the hurt and move on to atone for all the wrongs I've done. I'm not looking to go back on the streets to do wrong or harm." Johnny lifts his index finger, pointing with conviction. "Although I will do whatever is needed to get my family back together and keep them together. That's all I want."

Joel is deeply touched and believes Johnny is sincere.

When the time is up, six guards approach the conference room with shackles, cuffs, and chains. Johnny sees the look on Joel's face and grins. "Come on, guys, you're making me feel like Hannibal Lector."

"It's for your safety, not ours, jerk-off!" one of the guards says.

"I'll remember that," Johnny says.

The guard looks stunned that Johnny singled him out, but he puts on a tough front. "Are you threatening me, Ciminetti?"

Johnny smiles. "Not at all, and especially not in front of my lawyer." He leans in close, so Joel can't hear. "You fucking punk motherfucker. You're mine."

Johnny gives him a murderous stare, causing the guard to break out in a cold sweat. The guard swallows hard. "Just hold out your hands so we can cuff you, prisoner."

Johnny continues staring at the guard all the way back to his cell. The guard quits the next day. Two days later, he moves to Canada.

Joel now has a renewed vigor to win Johnny's freedom. He knows he must convince his rabbi and his family that he is taking the correct path by trying to help Johnny. He realizes it will be tough, but he is determined to do it.

8

GETTING SPUN IN RASHID'S WEB

Lena Jensen is the first one off a Greyhound bus from Iowa to New York City. She's wearing denim shorts and a mint-green T-shirt. At just nineteen years old, she is a rare beauty, a clean, wholesome, light-skinned, exotic, and exceptionally attractive African American girl seeking fame and fortune in the Big Apple. Her Afro hairstyle, which spikes out in different directions, gives her a modern, contemporary look, adding to her alluring and sensual vibe. All aspects indicate she has it all going on. Her deep, large, round ice-blue eyes are unusual, but they fit in perfectly with her fresh, clear, youthful, complexion. Her face could grace the cover of any fashion magazine. Her fine facial features and pouty lips are intoxicatingly sensual. Her eye-catching, solid, five-foot-ten-inch frame is perfect for runway modeling. Her long legs are fit and muscular but very feminine. She is special.

Lena knew something was different about her when boys in high school started falling all over themselves just to gawk at her. Many stuttered when trying to say hello. Most girls shunned her out of jealousy. Her male teachers, plus one female, tried seducing her even at the risk of losing their jobs. Her parents had to step in to warn two of them that their actions would be reported to the principal.

Looking for stardom, Lena has always longed to go to New York and be discovered. She finally mustered up enough courage, gathered a few things, saved a bit of money, and took the cheapest way to New York, which is what brought her to the bus terminal.

Rashid is looking for a new girl for his stable of prostitutes. A fresh, exotic girl to replace one of his old girls, who, in her despair, committed suicide by deliberately overdosing, feeling there was no hope left. She had given up the thought of ever getting away and felt death was the only escape from the hands of this true soldier of Satan.

Rashid sits in an outdoor café two blocks up from the bus station, on the corner of 50th Street and 8th Avenue. He positions himself like a spider that has spun a web, hoping to catch an unsuspecting victim. Pimps are not allowed in the bus terminal, because their recruitment tactics are well documented and reported by states all over the US. Many runaways have fallen prey to the charm and generosity of pimps, who exploit them into a life of prostitution. Rashid is smart and aware, so to go undetected, he sets up shop at the corner deli, and Lena is headed straight for it. He spots her as soon as she steps inside his web. Like a spider, he waits to wrap her in a cocoon.

Lena sits down at a table outside the deli that gives her a clear view of the goings-on around her. He makes his way toward her and sits at the next table.

Rashid is well dressed in his ghetto-chic outfit, thuggish but stylish, including a studded New York Yankees baseball cap, expensive jeans, short-sleeved shirt, and $500 sneakers, all top designer names. His jewelry is also gangster inspired, a look he knows is familiar to girls like Lena from watching rap videos on MTV.

Ordering soup and bottled water, she sits and stares at the world of New York City. Looking at the skyscrapers and traffic whizzing by, she is floored, still unable to believe she is there. She hopes to be discovered immediately.

"Is this your first time here?" Rashid asks in his slight gangster-hood accent, pulling her out of her daydream.

Stunned that a stranger is talking to her, she turns to him. "Yes, it is. It's so amazing. I can't believe I'm actually here."

Rashid seems like someone who is comfortable in his own skin. This is her first time speaking to a real gangster-looking black male, and it excites her. He acts just like the people in the music videos. She notices how he approached her with such ease and without any insecurity. She finds it attractive. She wants to hear more from him.

He takes off his hat. His neatly shaved haircut leaves a stubble look across his scalp, causing it to gleam slightly in the sun. His stylish razor-part running down the right side of his scalp is perfectly straight. His fine features and soulful eyes give him a trusting appearance. "I have to give you a lot of credit, being alone and coming from a different place far away." His remark is intended to see if she is alone.

"I know, right?" she says, free and unguarded. "I came all the way from Iowa, and I don't even know anyone here."

The waitress brings the bill to Lena's table, but Rashid snatches it out of her hand. "Here, let me get that for you." He flashes a thick roll of $100 bills.

Lena's eyes light up. Is he a famous rapper or a rich rap mogul? She has never seen that kind of money and jewelry being flaunted before.

Rashid grins, like a spider having just sunk its fangs into its victim. "Let's get out of here, girl, and get you some real food."

She is trusting and naïve. Her instincts tell her he is a nice person. After all, the rap videos and movies can't be wrong.

Believing she has made her first friend in New York, she walks with him to a parking garage.

"Wait right here," he says.

Moments later, a flashy, white four-door Bentley with wide tires and chrome wheels and trim pulls up. She is awestruck. His seduction is taking root. She is falling deeper into his web as he weaves it even tighter.

Rashid drives her across town to the East Side Highway and pulls up in front of the Water Club. It has an amazing view of the East River and is fancy, old New York dining at its best.

Rashid steps out of the car and hands the parking attendant a $50 bill. "Keep it close."

The attendant nods and smiles. "Yes. Will do!"

As they walk through the main dining area, Lena is floored by the amazing view of the East River through the large plate-glass windows. She sees huge yachts and small recreational vessels as well as larger boats filled with tourists. It takes her breath away.

Rashid hands the hostess a $100 bill. She looks at it and then smiles. "Your table is ready, sir." She seats them at the best table in the restaurant.

Rashid orders the surf and turf for two and a bottle of Cristal champagne.

Once their meal arrives and they begin to eat, he nods at Lena. "Is that all you have to wear?" He gestures to the windows, where daylight is turning to dusk. "It gets cold here at night."

She smiles uncomfortably, looking down at her shirt. "Well, this and two other pairs of shorts and shirts."

He shakes his head while pouring her a third glass of champagne. "I like what I see in you. I want you to work with me."

"What would I be doing?" she asks excitedly.

He smiles. "I'll give you a manager's position. It pays well, and it's

31

only part-time, so you can still pursue your modeling career. It's a perfect match."

Lena frowns. "How did you know I wanted to be a model?"

Rashid chuckles. "Someone as beautiful as you, why else would you be here?"

Flattered, Lena blushes, falling deeper into his cocoon of darkness.

"Hey, I just remembered. I have to take a quick ride up to the Bronx. Would you like to come? I won't be long."

Lena wipes her mouth with her linen napkin. "Where's the Bronx?"

Rashid's eyes widen. "What? You don't even know—never mind. It's not far from here. We'll be back in fifteen minutes."

"I guess," she says, glancing at her empty plate, feeling wary but also feeling a sense of obligation after the expensive meal.

"Great. I'll get the check. You'll love the Bronx. I have to stop off at my grandmother's apartment and bring her some food. I'll order her something now."

Riding back up to the Bronx, he makes a call. "Hey, Grandma, I'm on the way. I brought you your favorite food. I'll be there in about fifteen minutes. Please let me in. Okay, bye. I love you."

Rashid and Lena arrive at the front of his apartment building. Lena is frightened once she sees the neighborhood. It is dark and getting late. She wants to run but feels unsure.

Rashid rings the buzzer, and the front door of his building opens. She gets a sick feeling in the pit of her stomach with each step they take into the building. He knocks on the door to an apartment. It opens, but no one is there. She is frozen in fear. She wants to run, but before she can, he takes her hand and leads her inside.

Once the door closes behind him, Rashid grabs Lena's arms and slips a gag over her mouth. He calls his boys to come out. Two men join him to restrain her. She tries to scream, but the gag stifles her cries.

One of his boys runs a lighter under a large spoon filled with black-tar heroin. As it melts into a liquid, he fills a syringe with enough to get her and another person high. He injects himself first, sticking the needle into one of his veins near his elbow. Then he reaches for her arm. She struggles but her other captors hold her down. The needle rips through her skin and into her vein. He pushes down on the syringe and empties it into her. Lena is terrified.

Her shock and fear lead to uncontrolled shaking, her body gripped in fear as they rip her shorts and panties away. They brutally rape and sodomize her. The heroin takes effect, but she is still conscious of what is happening. She fights with pure adrenaline as they hold her down and take turns violating every orifice.

The gang of three keeps her high on heroin as they continue to rape her and strip away any sense of innocence, forever. As the heroin high becomes stronger, she loses her will to fight, her spirit broken.

This continues for four days until she is hooked and looking for the needle to inject herself. Rashid calls it "breaking the Mustang." He and his friends high-five each other, knowing she will need heroin to keep her addiction satisfied, and soon they will have her turning tricks and making money.

After breaking her in, they throw Lena into a room with Reggie, who begins to care for Lena. They form a bond and talk about how it's going to be over soon and how their lives will be normal with families of their own, and somehow it will be better. They hold hands and pretend that what they are doing is not really happening, that it's a bad dream that plays itself over and over, one they will wake from soon.

Reggie teaches Lena how to pray to the Virgin Mary, as Philomena taught her to do when Reggie was a young girl. They hope Mary will hear their prayers and answer them.

9

THEN THE DOOR WILL NOT STAY CLOSED

Joel's motion is set to be heard by a three-judge panel in New York City's State Supreme Court building in lower Manhattan on Tuesday at 10 a.m., leaving Joel only two days to convince his father to let him continue his quest to help Johnny. He will not proceed without his father's consent, but his father will not budge. Rabbi Spitz filled Joel's father in on the matter as soon as Calvin and Bulldog left his office.

"Rabbi, please reason with Joel, and have him forget this idea," Joel's father said. "I don't like that such people in power have come to you and asked for your help. It must be something that will lead to more trouble, and Joel will be in the middle of it. I don't like it."

He asked the rabbi not to tell Joel that they had spoken. "But, if need be, use the fact that you would call me to seek my guidance on this matter for leverage purposes."

Joel's father knows he cannot say no to Joel or any of his causes. He is a pushover for anything Joel asks of him. He loves Joel more than any of his other children. Joel is his heart. But he is sticking to his guns. Joel has called him night after night, asking him to reconsider. Joel has never met such fierce determination from his father. He is disheartened, but he is waiting for a reprieve.

On Tuesday morning, a three-judge panel convenes to hear Joel's oral argument. One is an elderly, dignified man with a gray horseshoe of hair around his head, Judge Frank Santoro. The second is a middle-aged African American man with a full head of salt-and-pepper hair and a round face, Judge Aaron White. The third is a tall, lanky man with a full head of gray hair and a thin hawkish nose, Judge Sol Klein. All three take a seat at the podium.

"The State of New York versus John Ciminetti," the bailiff says, reading the docket number.

Calvin looks around and smiles, because he doesn't see Joel in the courtroom. He thinks his visit to Joel's rabbi did the trick. He tenses when an Orthodox Jewish man wearing a yarmulke enters the court and then relaxes when he realizes it isn't Joel. He turns and smiles at Bulldog, who is standing next to him. "I thought that was him," he whispers.

Bulldog smiles and releases a sigh of approval. "Thank God it's not."

Johnny is led into court, shackled and with an escort of twelve court officers surrounding him. Judge Aaron White asks them to unshackle the prisoner. The captain in charge of the detail shakes his head in disbelief and then orders his officers to do as the judge requested.

Calvin watches as they unshackle Johnny. He never thought he would see Johnny again, and now he is fighting to keep him in prison.

"Where is your lawyer?" Judge Santoro asks.

Johnny shrugs. "I don't know, Your Honor. He was supposed to be here."

Judge Santoro scowls. "Well, if he doesn't show, we will dismiss your case, and then you will have to appeal it."

As the three judges confer quietly amongst themselves, Calvin feels elated. Then the elder of the three judges, Judge Santoro, looks at Johnny. "We have a lot of cases to be heard, Mr. Ciminetti, so we are going to have to—"

"Your Honor!" a voice calls from the back of the room. "Joel Rosenbaum, representing the defendant John Ciminetti."

A concert of relieved sighs goes up from Johnny's family members and supporters, who are there to show their support.

Calvin's jaw drops, and Bulldog shakes his head, a look of disappointment on his face.

Judges Klein and Santoro scold Joel for being late. It turns out he got an "okay" from his dad at 9:15 a.m. and had to be in court at 10:00 a.m. He sped all the way from the Bronx to lower Manhattan, making it in record time but was still late.

Judge Santoro scolds Joel for his tardiness. "Mr. Rosenbaum, you had better stop wasting any more of the court's time. Are you ready?"

"Yes, I am, your honor."

The judge puts on a large smile. "Oh how nice of you." He then fumes. "Then go ahead and start now!"

Joel quickly takes his notes out of his briefcase. "Your honor, at the time, Mr. Jones was not the district attorney of Bronx County but a young prosecutor working for the same office who questioned Mr. Ciminetti in a police station." Joel raises his eyes above his glasses and looks directly at three-judge panel. "Highly unusual." Then he breaks his stare and continues with his oral argument. "Mr. Ciminetti was not read his Miranda rights, specifically his most important right in this instant, his right to have an attorney present during questioning. Mr. Jones coerced Mr. Ciminetti into admitting that the gun found at the scene was his. He told Mr. Ciminetti that if he would admit to owning the gun, he would not be implicated in the crime and would be free to leave and nothing further would happen to him. So, unfortunately for Mr. Ciminetti, after days of questioning and constant badgering and the police applying pressure, not giving him any time or opportunity to sleep, their tactics took their toll. Mr. Ciminetti signed an affidavit admitting that the gun was his. Then Mr. Jones informed Mr. Ciminetti that the bullets in the gun were forensically matched, and he would be charged with murder.

"This is a flagrant violation of Miranda and a total disregard for the rule of law. Your honor, it's for these reasons that society has lost its trust in our police. These unlawful tactics are why the police are under attack! Frankly, your honor, we deserve better than this, especially from the Bronx County District Attorney's office. Their entire existence is to uphold the law, not break it.

"Mr. Ciminetti is rightfully seeking the relief in his appellate brief to this court that, without question, should be afforded to him. Mr. Jones deliberately did not inform Mr. Ciminetti of his rights. The members of this honorable court surely recognize this as a travesty of justice and an unlawful conviction that cannot be allowed to stand. It is this astute body's duty to expeditiously undo the wrong that was perpetrated on Mr. Ciminetti some twenty-four years ago. His basic rights to a fair trial were totally compromised. The conduct displayed by Mr. Jones is unconscionable and unbecoming of an elite prosecutor. For this reason, Mr. Ciminetti's conviction should be overturned and vacated by granting him the relief he so justly deserves. Your honor, Mr. Ciminetti has served twenty-four years of his first sentence, which is more than enough time to satisfy the restitution that was required of him. He must be set free if this sentence is vacated."

Joel's anger flares as he reaches his conclusion. "In regard to this court's decision in this case, the astute members of this body should join Mr. Ciminetti in demanding that this kind of conduct never be used again, nor shall it be tolerated in a society governed by laws."

Joel raises a clenched fist and extends his index finger as he waves his hand around like a swashbuckler. "This court must send a loud and clear message that resonates through the legal system. If this is their brand of justice, we'll have none of it!"

Joel, visibly upset, angrily walks back to his chair and sits down next to Johnny, ending his argument. The courtroom is stunned into silence. It is finally broken by Judge Klein, who nods at Calvin. "Mr. Jones, it's your turn."

Still reeling from the shock of Joel being there, Calvin takes a quick breath. "Thank you, Your Honor. Mr. Ciminetti was convicted of two murders twenty-four years ago, brutal and heinous crimes. Neither of the victims' heads were ever recovered. If he is freed, he will surely kill again for one reason and one reason only—he loves it. He gets a charge out of it, almost like a sexual release. He is addicted to it, and he needs it, like regular people need oxygen. He is a serial killer."

Judge White pauses the proceedings and orders the court officers to put Johnny back in shackles and not to take them off until he is well out of the court building.

"I trust you have read my brief in answer to Mr. Ciminetti's motion," Calvin continues.

"Yes," Judge Santoro replies. "But it is actually very weak compared to the defense motion for his release. Your reasoning and answers are non-compelling. You need to make an argument here and now to persuade the court if you hope to succeed in your opposition."

Calvin is dumbfounded, completely unprepared for such a response. He thought Joel wouldn't show. His last conversation with the rabbi was that he was sure Joel would not be there.

"Your Honor," he says finally, "if you have read the case law in the State's answer to the defendant's motion, you will agree that it clearly shows that Mr. Ciminetti should not be released."

The two older judges, Klein and Santoro, shake their heads in disbelief. Judge Klein is upset with Calvin, especially after giving him a call. "I am giving you one last chance to make a better argument for yourself, Mr. Jones," Judge Klein says. You are running a high risk of losing."

Calvin looks at the floor, as if to concede defeat. "The State has no choice but to stand by its written answer to the Ciminetti motion."

"Your Honor, may I speak?" Joel asks, eager to get a word in.

Judge Klein sneers at him. "No, you may not."

Joel stares at him in disbelief. "But I'm defending my client, Your Honor. You have to let me speak."

"It will not be necessary," Judge Klein replies.

Joel hears a murmur from Johnny's family members. He looks back at them and puts a finger to his lips, motioning them to be quiet. He knows something big is about to happen.

The courtroom is silent as Judge Santoro speaks. "The case law that the State has alluded to in its answer to the defense's motion only cuts against them and in favor of the defendant, as pointed out by the defense. Therefore, as much as we do not want to do this, we have no choice in this matter, bound by the law. We are not going to make Mr. Ciminetti wait for our written answer. We will render our decision now. Mr. Jones, we find in favor of the defendant's motion and grant the relief he is seeking: time served on his first charge of murder, and we are vacating the conviction of the second. We also order his immediate release. Mr. Ciminetti, unfortunately, you are free to go."

Cheers and applause erupt in the courtroom. Judge Santoro bangs his gavel.

Calvin rises to his feet. "Your Honor, do you know what you're doing here?"

Judge Klein bangs his gavel again and then points it at Calvin. "Consider yourself lucky the defendant does not have you disbarred. You did it, Calvin, and you know it: prosecutorial misconduct. This court is adjourned."

Judge White bangs his gavel for a final time as the three judges rise and walk out through a door behind the podium. There is bedlam in the courtroom as Johnny's family and supporters cry, laugh, hug, applaud, and kiss each other. Some of them raise their fist to Johnny in a victory salute.

Philomena is crying, comforted by her girlfriends and family.

Johnny looks around, feeling triumphant as the officers remove his handcuffs. Not seeing Reggie anywhere in the courtroom, his mood dims somewhat. He senses something is not right.

Joel feels amazing. He smiles as Johnny's family and friends besiege him, congratulating him on a job well done.

Bulldog locks his eyes on Joel and walks across the front of the courtroom to confront him. "You really think you did something good, Rosenbaum?" He smirks. "Wait and see what your client does. I want to know how you feel then, when you see the faces of the family members of his next victims. You did nothing here but let a defective, deranged maniac go free. I hope you feel good about yourself."

He walks away, pointing at Johnny on his way out. "We'll be watching you, psycho! Just try it! We will take you the fuck out, you murdering motherfucker."

Johnny stares back and smiles, following him out the door with his eyes. "I'm sorry if I ruined your day, Detective!"

Johnny grins. He grabs Joel, wraps him in a hug, and plants a kiss on his cheek. "I don't know how to thank you, but if there is anything I can ever do for you, let me know."

Joel is saddened by the detective's remarks as he sticks papers into his briefcase. He pauses and looks at Johnny. "Yes, there is something you can do for me. Prove that detective wrong. I don't want to be sorry for getting you out."

"I promise. I won't do anything to anyone. I will just protect my family—at any cost."

Joel looks at Johnny. "As crazy as this may sound, I'm pleased to hear that."

The kick in the face, the bloody nose, and the racially charged insults Rashid hurled at him are never far from his mind. He grins to himself. *Let the games begin.*

10

Johnny Helps Joel Out

After all the adulation has died down in the courtroom, Joel offers to give Johnny a ride home. "You and I can go over the aspects of your release. We have to stop off at the Bronx courthouse first though."

Johnny, feeling amazing as he takes his first steps as a free man, simply smiles and nods. "Okay, sure."

On the way home from the Bronx courthouse, on the Grand Concourse, driving through the bustling streets of a large, mostly Hispanic area, Johnny asks Joel to pull over in front of a *bodega* (a Spanish grocery store).

Joel gives him a concerned look. "This is not the greatest neighborhood for a Jew with a yarmulke."

"Don't worry," Johnny says. "You think these people are going to notice you?"

Joel nods. "Well, yes, I do."

"Don't worry," Johnny assures him. "I'll be right back."

Johnny goes inside and gets in line at the cash register, waiting to buy cigarettes.

As Joel waits outside, he watches the children across the street playing in the water that is being provided by a sprinkler cover attached to a fire hydrant, keeping the kids cool in the summer heat.

Suddenly, he hears a tap on his window. He turns toward it and sees a gun. Fear reverberates throughout his body, and his heart beats quickly, triggering his nervous system and making him feel weak. The person holding the gun, a tall, skinny albino black man dressed in ragged clothes with an unkempt blonde Afro and a face ravaged by acne, motions for Joel to roll down his window. Joel obeys his command.

As the man opens his mouth, he exposes rotten teeth, caused by the various drugs he uses. He looks like a zombie. "Give me all your money, motherfucker, or I'll put a cap in your brain."

Joel reaches for his wallet and holds it out to the man. As the man reaches for the wallet, he is yanked away. A loud bang rings in Joel's ears as the gun goes off, and a bullet shatters the passenger window of his car. The children playing in the water and other pedestrians scatter in fear.

Johnny struggles with the man for his gun, which is pointing at Johnny's face. He manages to redirect the barrel slightly right before the gun fires again, just missing Johnny's face. The bullet crashes into the front window of the *bodega*, shattering it. The store owner, who was watching the action until then, runs and ducks for cover.

Johnny grabs the albino by his genitals, causing him to cry out in pain. He tries to stick his finger in Johnny's eye, but Johnny repositions his face to receive the man's finger in his mouth and clamps down with his teeth. A clunking noise is heard as Johnny bites the man's finger clean off.

The albino drops his gun and clutches his hand, screaming in pain. Johnny tosses the gun into the backseat of Joel's car as the albino falls to his knees in anguish.

Johnny opens the passenger door of Joel's car, gets in, and then spits the man's finger out the window.

For Joel, it seems like he is watching it in slow motion as the man's finger travels, end over end, landing on top of the albino, who is still screaming as he clutches his bleeding hand.

The man's finger bounces off the albino and falls onto the sidewalk right next to the pool of blood coming from the albino's hand.

"Move!" Johnny yells.

"Maybe we should wait for the police," Joel says, still in shock. In response, Johnny leans over, puts the car in gear, and steps on the gas. Steering the car with one hand, the car skids and fishtails out of the area. Now Joel knows why Johnny is considered a maniac, but he is grateful to Johnny for saving him.

11

JOEL SAYS GOODBYE TO A JOB WELL DONE

Joel is back at his apartment packing his car with some boxes and things to make room for Johnny. His canon law classes ended two weeks earlier. He is moving to another trial in New England, in the town of Cape Cod, defending a minister who leads a small flock. He is accused of killing a parishioner. Prosecutors believe he committed the murder based on his interpretation of canon law. Joel welcomes the challenge.

Joel feels a bit sad to leave Philomena. They have grown close. "Well, Philomena, I'm happy to see you are looking well these days. I'm going to miss you and your cooking."

Philomena smiles. "I'm so thankful to you for giving me my family back. If there is ever anything I can do for you, please let me know."

Tilting his head, he grins. "Well, yes there is. If you wouldn't mind, would you make me one of those Italian-kosher meals next time I'm in New York?"

Philomena smiles. "Of course! You can have as many as you like, anytime you feel like. My door is always open."

Joel smiles gratefully. "You're too kind."

Johnny waits until his mom is finished. Then he approaches Joel with a hug. Stepping back Johnny sighs, "If it weren't for you, I would have rotted away in jail. I don't know how I can ever pay you back."

Joel smiles. "I can tell you how."

Johnny gives him an inquisitive look. "How?"

Joel's face turns serious. "Stay out of jail."

Johnny smiles. "I concur with you on that one."

Johnny accompanies Joel out to his car. The two men give a final hug. Then Joel gets in and leaves for New England.

12

JOHNNY LEARNS THE TRUTH ABOUT REGGIE

"Mom, tell me what's going on with Reggie. Why haven't you brought her to see me? You told me she was away at school. I know that's not true. What aren't you telling me?"

Philomena breaks down in tears. "I don't want you to get in trouble. I need you to be here."

"Tell me what it is now, Ma!"

Philomena's body heaves with a huge sigh. "She is with a pimp and is hooked on heroin. The pimp threatens her and beats her. She's too scared to leave. She says he's threatened to hurt me and . . . Reggie's baby."

Johnny's eyes go wide. "Her what?"

Philomena explains further. "Reggie had a baby with the pimp, and the baby lives with me in the house."

Johnny shakes his head slowly and bites his bottom lip, clasping his hands in front of him. The news devastates him, eclipsing his victory. He presses his mother for more details. Philomena senses Johnny fading from her, a coldness overtaking over him. His stare becomes dark and deep. It's a look Philomena knows well—and fears. It's the same look Johnny would drift into as a little boy, absorbed into his thoughts, which would consume him for long periods of time. When he came back, she would ask him, "Where did you drift off to?" He would never reply. As he became a teenager, that same look would appear. Soon after, the police would alert her that Johnny was arrested and ask her to come get Johnny out of jail. As he became a young man, it was the last look she saw when he left her house and went to jail for twenty-four years.

Philomena places her hands on both sides of Johnny's face. "Look at me!" she screams in hopes of him not going to that place inside. "Please, it's God. He brought you back to me. Don't do anything. He will make everything right again. I need you in my life. Your daughter needs you in hers. Don't let this take you away from us again." She begins to cry, knowing she can't control him.

Johnny releases her grip, causing her hands to drop to her side. His coldness, a calling from the one below, will not be denied. It has gripped his innermost being. It leads him away from her and toward the basement door. His raging focus is on getting Reggie back. His thoughts of causing death excite him. He craves his dance with the devil in one of his many familiar rituals of death. It blasts inside of him. A twisted fatherly instinct that runs through him causes an explosive, toxic cocktail made from a sadistic recipe of mayhem and murder. An adrenaline rush of power and an unbridled, undeniable demonic possession ignites, causing an energy field that needs to be let out of him.

He trudges down the basement stairs. When he reaches the bottom of the stairs, he pulls on an old-fashioned light chain. A dim bulb illuminates the dark, cold basement. He reaches for a crowbar and uses it to scrape against the old cement wall. It loosens, and pieces of old cement begin to fall. He works harder. The crowbar causes sparks to fly from its tip, moving faster still, until the shape of a large compartment appears. He reaches inside and frees a large drawer from its hidden compartment. Johnny opens it, revealing an arsenal. He reaches a climatic release of energy when he sees his old tools of death consisting of revolvers, a machine gun, a sawed-off shotgun, boxes of ammo, knives of all shapes and sizes, blackjacks, brass knuckles, and disguises, all tools of his old craft when on the streets doing hits for the mob and stickups with his criminal friends. He pulls out a fat woman's suit, lays it on the floor, and urinates on it. Then he puts on makeup and a gray wig with a bun.

Having to sneak past the twenty-four-hour surveillance by the NYPD detectives, he slips out of his house in the dead of night through a skylight in his roof. He jumps from rooftop to rooftop and then climbs down and runs down back alleys.

When he reaches the street, he assumes a hunched appearance, like an old woman with poor posture, limping slightly. He carries a shopping bag. It is unusual to see an old lady walking the streets at 1:30 a.m., but his urine smell will ward off anyone who might want to bother him.

He gets to 187th Street and walks toward Crotona Avenue. When he reaches the corner, he walks on the opposite side of the street from where his daughter is being held. He sees a tall black man with two companions dealing drugs and taking money. From Philomena's description of her granddaughter's captor, Johnny's keen eye and his street smarts tell him it is Rashid.

He crosses the street and hobbles past the building, taking mental notes of the area, including the courtyard. As he walks by, the two men with Rashid stare at him.

"Damn, Grandma, you smell like an elephant's asshole," one of them says.

"Why do you go around smelling elephant's asses?" Johnny mutters in an old lady's voice. "Don't you know you can get diseases doing that?"

The other gang members laugh at their friend. "Oh, shit, homeboy, that old bitch done fucked you up!"

Just then, Reggie appears, bringing the proceeds she received from her last trick for Rashid. "Three hundred," she says over the laughter.

Johnny hears her voice and whips his head around. He and Reggie lock eyes. The men are spooked by the quick spin of the old lady's head and by the concentrated and radiating stare from the old lady's face. It's frightfully eerie.

"Daddy!" Reggie shrieks. Then she passes out, hitting the ground.

Rashid looks at Reggie. "Bitch! What are you trippin' on me? You stupid motherfucker, get up!" He slaps her face.

Johnny feels unbridled rage and wants to react, but he maintains his composure and continues his recon mission, studying every detail. He knows the area well. These are the same streets and alleys he played in as a kid. His memories of those days are still vivid.

Johnny returns home and plots how to get his beloved, his one and only daughter, away from her hellish captors and back with his family. He knows he must plan every last detail to avoid detection and prosecution. He will have to do it right under the noses of NYPD's best homicide detectives. It will not be an easy task, but he is a smart, skillful killer whose thoughts are laser focused.

His plan takes its final shape. He will eliminate his daughter's tormenters and get away with it. He salivates at the thought of what's to come.

Little did Reggie and Lena realize their prayers were being heard. But if they knew what forces their prayers were about to unleash onto the mean streets of the Bronx, their teeth would chatter, and their bodies would shiver. It will seem like the help they seek has come not from heaven but straight from hell.

13

FIRST STRIKE

Michelle's Retreat is the "in" place for the hip-hop and rap crowd in Mt. Vernon, New York. Owner Salvatore Guido started as a bouncer and slowly took over as Michelle got older and retired. His changes to the once cheap and dingy strip club are grand and luxurious. Guido handpicks the dancers. His taste for women varies. Most are of Latin descent, with a small contingent of white and black girls. All the girls have a certain look to them. Healthy, round bodies and full backsides are a must. To stay number one in the strip club business, he pays some of the biggest names in the rap and hip-hop world to make appearances, drinking Cristal and hanging out in the private back rooms throughout the night. He provides anything they desire in the way of drugs and booze.

It is also the place where pimps go to show off their girls, like cattle ranchers showing their livestock to potential buyers. The showcase is for potential johns to see the pimps' merchandise and to meet up later at a location the pimp provides.

Inside, the bar is surrounded by a long, elevated runway, the main stage, lined with colored florescent lighting. Evenly spaced in the middle of the runway are three stripper poles. The flooring is parquet wood, so the girls can move about easily.

Both sides of the bar have spaces for thirsty customers who are anxious to see the girls and check out the pimps' latest "stock." Two elevated runway platforms with lounges run down both sides of the bar area, with three steps leading up to them, and smaller birdcage stages are scattered about the platforms.

Michelle's Retreat is also the meeting place for the local street thrugs and the pimps, who are partners in their prostitution and drug-dealing empire. A few unscrupulous members of the organization all deny it and preach against it and make like they deplore such business, but as the money comes in, they are sure to have their hands out, so they can line their pockets.

Some of these well-known men are friends of Johnny's from the old neighborhood, before he went away. They include a father-and-son team, Large Louis, a tall, muscular man with a full head of floppy hair, and his son, Frankie, who resembles an accountant rather than a gangster. With his wire-rimmed glasses and youthful look, it is apparent that Frankie does not belong in that environment, but he begged his father to get him inducted into the organization. It took some doing, but Louis was finally able to make it happen by calling in some serious favors and paying people in high positions to get it done. Now they are both "made men," members of an organized crime family. They frequent Michelle's to meet their pimps and drug dealers, to get their cut of money, and to sample the prostitutes' wares.

Rashid enters Michelle's with Reggie on one arm and Lena on the other. Frankie sees Reggie and is instantly infatuated. He knows he can have her because of his dad's status with Rashid. Her amazing body—tall frame, protruding buttocks, and round breasts—is more than he can stand. He leans over to Large Louis and points at Reggie. "Dad, can I have her?"

Louis looks at her and nods. "Not bad. That's Johnny Ciminetti's daughter. I remember her when she was a kid. Wait a little bit. We'll do her and her girlfriend together."

Rashid hands Louis a stack of $100 bills. "Thirty-two thousand," he says. "It's all there."

Large Louis looks at the stack and smiles. "You did good, kid. Rashid, send your two girls into the back office. Me and my son want to have some time with them."

"Sure, no problem Louis."

Outside, an old, blind man clutching a shopping bag with roses protruding from it and feeling his way around with a cane asks to be let in to sell his roses. The large, portly African American doorman with a huge Afro has a four-pronged fork comb hanging from his hair. He decides who gets in and searches them for weapons. He's tough, but he has a heart, and he sees no problem with letting the old man into the club. Little does he realize the old man with wavy gray hair is not interested in selling flowers. He is interested in only two things: Rashid and Reggie.

That's because the old man is really Johnny in disguise.

Inside, he recognizes Large Louis from the old days and remembers his son, Frankie, as a little boy. He watches as Rashid leads Lena and Reggie into the back office, followed by Louis and Frankie, who is carrying an open bottle of Dom Perignon. The old man drops his shopping bag on the floor and walks out.

As soon as he is outside, a massive explosion erupts behind him, blowing out the club's front window.

Louis runs out of the back office, Frankie in tow. People are shaken as they lift themselves off the floor, stunned. Sirens can already be heard in the distance, as the police and the fire department respond to the call.

Guido's temper flares as he looks around for who could have detonated such a powerful device, which blew down most of his ceiling, along with his front window.

Large Louis wants to leave Michelle's before the police arrive, but Frankie is reluctant, still thinking about the girls. His father yanks his arm. "Let's go, now!"

With a concerned expression on his face, Frankie follows, still looking back at the office for Reggie.

Large Louis is no fool. He knows exactly who is to blame without even seeing him. He knows he has a problem with Johnny Ciminetti.

Johnny waits on a rooftop where he can survey Rashid's building. He watches as Rashid leads his boys, Reggie, and Lena back into his apartment. Daybreak is coming. He must get back before the light of day betrays his clandestine activities.

He jumps from fire escapes to back alleys, recalling his youth. In his childhood, he used to run through the same back alleys to make it home in time for dinner or risk facing the wrath of his father, who would take off his belt and administer harsh and vicious discipline, which only intensified Johnny's ferocity in later years. Finally, he slips back in through the skylight, the NYPD detectives parked outside unaware of his nightly excursions.

At 8 a.m., the doorbell rings. The portly, hotheaded detective, Bulldog, along with a tall, well-built, red-haired, green-eyed freckled detective, Patrick Murphy, a captain from Bronx homicide division, are standing at the front door. Bulldog asks Philomena if he can speak to Johnny.

"Wait a second," she says. "I'll go get him."

Johnny comes down to greet them. Having just returned home two hours earlier, he is groggy but keenly aware, playing the role of the innocent. "Oh, how are you, my friend?" he says when he sees Bulldog. "Last time I saw you was back at the courthouse."

"Fuck you, psycho!" Bulldog says. "You better move out of New York, you murdering motherfucker, because we will always be following you, and when you make your move, even if you surrender, you'll be in a body bag."

Johnny smirks. "You guys didn't even bring me any coffee this morning? I mean, I would have brought you some."

Mafucci grinds his teeth. "Ciminetti, the only coffee you'll be getting will be recycled in the way of my piss in a cup, you scumbag."

Johnny frowns, appearing puzzled. "You seem very angry, Detective Mafucci. Perhaps you didn't have a bowel movement today. I think you need to take that dick out of your ass so you can shit."

Detective Murphy steps between Johnny and his partner before their confrontation reaches a boiling point.

Johnny smiles. "Enjoy the rest of your day, and thanks for stopping by."

"How's your daughter doing, John?" Bulldog yells over Murphy's shoulder as Murphy leads him away.

For a moment, Johnny's smile fades. The words hit him hard. He vows Rashid will suffer a bit more at the hour of his death.

14

FAMILY BONDING

Philomena calls her friend of fifty years, Mary, who has been caring for Reggie's daughter, and asks her to bring her great-granddaughter back home. "Johnny knows about her."

As Mary drops off the child, she studies Philomena's troubled face. "Is everything okay?"

Philomena shakes her head uncertainly. "I'm not sure of anything anymore."

Johnny lies in bed staring at the ceiling, plotting his next move, when he feels a strange presence in the house. Then he sees a flash past his door. Not sure what to make of it, he gets out of bed and hides himself in a strategic position in his room. Then he sees a small figure run back across his doorway, a small African American child.

"Ma, what is this?" he asks.

Philomena walks up the stairs and stands in his doorway, holding the little girl's hand. "This is your granddaughter. Her name is Philomena, after me. Reggie wanted that name for her."

Johnny's head spins with the series of events happening so close together. He looks at his granddaughter and then looks away. "Keep her away from me. I want nothing to do with her." He closes the door to his room.

Philomena's heart is broken upon hearing his words. "Her veins have your blood in them," she says, her eyes glistening with tears. "She is yours."

Her remarks are met by silence. Philomena gathers up the child and brings her downstairs, wiping away tears, then makes something for young Philomena to eat.

Later, Johnny is sitting on his front porch watching young children play in front of his house. Philomena brings his granddaughter out to play, and she immediately joins in the fun.

Moments later, Philomena's phone rings inside. It's an old-fashioned phone attached to the wall in her kitchen. "Watch her," she says, getting up to answer it, "I'll be right back."

Johnny looks disgusted at the request, and Philomena regards him sadly for a second before hurrying inside to get the phone.

Watching the crowd of children playing, Johnny sees his granddaughter trying to ride a scooter that belongs to one of the other girls. As she pushes off with her foot and begins to roll, the young girl and her older brother descend upon her. They throw young Philomena to the ground and hit her, giving her a bleeding nose in addition to a scraped knee.

Johnny jumps down from the porch and fetches his granddaughter. He pushes her two young assailants away, but the little boy refuses to stop.

"I'll give you a kick right up your ass," Johnny warns. The boy stops and begins to cry, running home. Johnny turns toward his front porch. "Ma! Come and get the kid! She got hurt."

Philomena drops the phone and runs out. "Oh my God, what happened?"

Annoyed, Johnny looks across the street and sees the boy come around the corner with his father, a large Hispanic man with a menacing look on his face.

"That's the man," the boy says, pointing at Johnny.

"What's your problem?" Johnny asks.

The man knows Johnny from jail. He quickly gathers his two children and leaves the area.

"Teach your kids how to play!" Johnny yells after him. "Your son is a bully."

The man keeps walking without looking back.

Johnny turns and sees Murphy and Bulldog are out of their car with their guns drawn, waiting for him to make a move toward the boy's father. They have orders to shoot to kill if Johnny is a danger to anyone.

"Better calm down, Ciminetti," Murphy says. "You're fixing to get yourself shot."

"Go ahead, psycho," Bulldog says. "I'd love nothing more than to empty this gun into your fucking head."

Johnny looks directly at him. "Go fuck your mother and your father for dropping a worthless load like you."

Bulldog peers down the barrel of his gun, aiming for a head shot. He is a hair away from dispensing his first bullet.

"Come inside," Philomena says, tugging Johnny with one arm while she holds her sobbing great-granddaughter in the other. When Johnny refuses to move, she tugs his arm again, harder this time. "I said, come inside."

Sneering at the detectives, Johnny obeys his mother's wishes.

Philomena places the crying child on the kitchen counter by the sink. Johnny finds it only natural to try and take the child's mind off what happened. As Philomena attends to his granddaughter's wounds, Johnny makes funny faces, with quick comical movements and sounds. Soon, he has young Philomena laughing hysterically.

Philomena gives the child a shower and dresses her wounds with disinfectant ointment and bandages. Then she puts her to sleep.

Johnny is lying in his bed when Philomena knocks and then opens his bedroom door to let him know she is going to bed. He acknowledges her with a nod. Then he turns over to sleep for the night.

A short time later, his eyes shoot open when he hears the hinges of his bedroom door creak. His granddaughter is standing in his doorway hugging her Build-A-Bear teddy bear. As Johnny pretends to sleep, she walks toward his bed, climbs in beside Johnny, and tucks herself under the covers, snuggling in beside him. He has never felt such emotions before and is overcome with unexpected love for his grandchild.

The next morning, a brand-new scooter is leaning against the front door. Johnny slipped out and brought it home for his granddaughter that night. Philomena tears up when she sees it, hugging and kissing him as she cries. "So, you want nothing to do with her, huh?"

"Okay, okay, all right, enough already with the kisses," he says, pushing her away gently.

She runs upstairs and returns a moment later with young Philomena, who is rubbing sleep from her eyes. The moment she sees the scooter, her face lights up. "Is it mine?"

"Yes, baby," Philomena says. "Your grandfather bought it for you." Young Philomena runs to Johnny and kisses and hugs him. "You're the best grandfather in the whole world. I love you."

Johnny is taken in hook, line, and sinker, and an unshakable bond is formed.

15

PAUL CONFRONTS EVIL

In Ciccarone Park, two blocks from Johnny's house, Mary, Philomena's closest friend, is sitting on a bench near where children are playing. She is waiting in case she has to bring young Philomena back to her house. As she sits there, she notices a young, tall, thin, wholesome-looking man with a neatly parted head of hair that nicely frames his handsome face. His lean body, clad in a long black robe, black sash, and with a priest's collar at his neck, seems to walk effortlessly toward Mary. He stops in front of her and bows his head in respect.

"Hello," he says.

She smiles slightly and nods. "Good afternoon, Father. It is such a lovely summer afternoon. I have not seen you at the Mount Carmel Church before. Are you new to the congregation?"

He responds with a slight smile as he stares into the sky, squinting at the sun. "No, I'm just visiting here from a far-away place."

Mary shifts her slightly overweight but still shapely body. Her dyed blonde hair mixes nicely with her natural hazel eyes. Her still-pretty face is adorned with high cheekbones, and her thin nose has a slight lump on the bridge of it. It gives her the air of an older but still sexy Italian movie star. "Are you on vacation, Father?" she asks, starting to wonder if he really is a priest.

The man chuckles as he looks at Mary. "You know, I can see you."

Mary looks at him, puzzled. "I know you can see me, sir. Are you really a priest?"

The young man grins in amazement. "Very clever. You are performing your deeds through the old lady's best friend. Who would have suspected?"

He sits on a bench facing the woman, separated by a small paved trail. He lifts his sleeves and then pulls out a handkerchief and dabs blood from open wounds between his wrists and palms. He has the gift of stigmata—the wounds suffered by Christ as he was nailed to the cross.

Mary's complexion turns gray, and a look of astonishment fills her face, her mouth falling open as her heart fills with fear. Then a chilling calm descends upon her. Her mouth closes, her wide eyes narrow, and an evil look fills her face. "Why are you here? There's nothing here for you. His soul belongs to us and all the powers of darkness."

The man pulls down his sleeves and puts away his hankie. "We have been summoned by the most powerful prayers to the Prince of Peace for his ultimate and divine intervention. He has been compelled to answer."

"Why his soul?" the demon that controls Mary's body asks. "He has done so much of my bidding. His soul has been with me for most of his life. He has done my work for me in the most ungodly ways. I am going to take his soul. He will commit more heinous and unspeakable acts against you in my name. I will blacken his soul, so you surely will not want it."

The young, handsome gentleman looks at the ground, watching ants gather around a piece of uneaten popsicle dropped by one of the children playing nearby. Then he refocuses on Mary. "The prayers said for him will not grant him automatic passage to heaven. He must perform two acts of unselfish love, and one of them must consist of the ultimate sacrifice for another here on Earth. If he does that, we will battle you for his soul."

A little boy runs past Mary. The demon inside of Mary makes her stick out her foot, tripping him and causing him to fall and get a deep gash on his forehead. Mary smiles at Paul as the boy's mother runs over to retrieve her child. Mary points to another couple with a child in the park. "It seems like that man, enjoying his afternoon with his family, is about to have a heart attack, and if he doesn't get immediate attention, he'll die."

A block away, an ambulance is driving when one of the paramedics rubs his stomach. "I just got an urge for an Italian wedge. Make a right turn here. There's a great Italian deli down this block."

As they park outside the deli, the crew, which consists of two young men and a young female, begins to gather their lunch order.

The man Mary pointed out is playing with his daughter on the swings when he feels bolts of shooting pain in his arm and shoulder.

He grasps for his heart as he falls to the ground and labors to breathe, falling unconscious.

His wife screams for help. A younger teenage boy sees the seriousness of the situation, runs to the ambulance, and bangs on the driver's door, yelling as he points toward the downed man and the woman kneeling beside him.

The paramedics spring into action and rush to the man and his distraught wife. After taking his vitals, they determine the seriousness of the situation, and one of the paramedics plunges an adrenaline-filled needle deep into the man's chest, right into the center of his heart, which has stopped beating.

"We have a pulse!" the female paramedic yells a moment later as the other two paramedics perform chest compressions and administer oxygen. The man's heart begins beating at a strong, fierce pace.

Paul looks back at Mary and smiles. "Well, I guess he's going to make it." He stands up.

As he walks away, he passes the male paramedic who first got the desire for an Italian wedge, Fernando, a stocky, macho-looking Hispanic man who sports a neatly cropped beard and a well-manicured haircut. Paul puts his hand on Fernando's shoulder. "Good job, Fernando!"

Fernando thinks nothing of it, because his name is on the ID tag attached to his chest pocket.

"It's a good thing you had an urge for an Italian wedge, or this unlucky fellow would never have made it." Paul smiles, revealing perfect teeth. "Try the Italian combo with the fresh mozzarella. I hear it's their best."

Fernando stares at him, perplexed. "Who are you?"

The young man smiles. "I am Paul." Then he strides back toward Mary.

"You can choose to let it play itself out and see if we feel he has completed his task for us and allow him into the kingdom, or you can do your dirtiest to stop it," he says to her. "We are confident you will do your absolute best to stop it."

The demon controlling Mary looks up at Paul. "I will, as will all the souls of the darkness. We will stop him from ever entering your kingdom. He is ours and will burn amongst the fires of eternal darkness. He is only one pathetic soul. Why are you putting so many resources into saving him?"

Paul smiles, reluctant to speak any longer with the corrupting demon. "It's the bigger picture, and you know what I'm talking about—your grandiose scheme—and we will stop it before it can hatch."

"Aren't you more worried about the souls in your church?" the demon asks. "Surely, they are much more valuable to you. So many are down under with me. Why have you not saved them?"

Paul's eyes flash with rage. "Our way, our time, and at our choosing. Get away from me, demon! Leave this woman's earthly body. It is so commanded by Christ himself. He demands this of you!"

The demon shakes Mary's head and pulls her lips back into a gruesome imitation of a smile. "No, I will not leave her."

Paul dips his index finger into the open wound on his left wrist and moves it toward Mary's forehead. She tries to wiggle away, but invisible angels hold her in position. With the blood of the holiest dripping from his finger, Paul draws the sign of the cross on Mary's forehead.

A deep darkness drapes the park as the powerful demon is driven out. A fierce wind whirls around, causing trees to fall.

The wind swoops toward Johnny's house, causing two manholes to explode, sending their covers high into the air before they crash down onto the hood and the roof of two parked cars. The hellish voice and the screeches of the fleeing demon tumble through the howling wind. "He is mine! He is ours! His soul is ours to keep, for eternity!"

16

WHO IS PAUL?

Paul is of one the highest-ranking members of a secretive order within the Catholic Church, the order of the *ticus sanguinem sanctorum et occultum societatem* (Secret Society of the Purest and Holiest Blood). However, his undying loyalty is to what many in the conspiracy world call the Black Pope, a man both feared and revered, who is committed to advancing the Roman Catholic agenda. He is committed to eliminating serious threats to destroy the Catholic Church, from outside or within. He believes such serious threats are directly derived from Satan and must be met with devastating force to be totally neutralized by any means . . . ensuring that they will not survive to present themselves again. His official title is the Superior General of the Jesuits, but he is also the unofficial leader of the Secret Society of the Purest and Holiest Blood. His name is Francisco Libatore. He believes Paul is guided directly by the Spirit of God and Christ. Both the Black Pope and the actual Pope feel Paul has been chosen for the gift of stigmata as well as the gift of bilocation (the ability to be in two places at once) and to receive visions of future events that will affect the survival of the Church and the world. Paul has been sent out into the world to stop negative future events before they happen. He confronts the forces of darkness that are behind the plots to destroy the Church, degrade its morality, and, ultimately, destroy the world by collapsing the Church and then bankrupting humankind of its morality.

Paul received his gift during his darkest moments on Earth, caused by a stolen and disrupted love affair. He and his girlfriend, Rita, were soul mates, happily intertwined in love and planning to get married. Suddenly, she left and wed another man, ignoring Paul's request to speak with her.

Unbeknownst to Paul, Rita's father disapproved of him and chose another man for her to marry. He became so obsessed and distraught in getting his way over ending their relationship, it made him physically ill, causing him to collapse and fall unconscious. Finally, out of guilt, Rita yielded to her father's demands.

Desperate to understand what happened, and unable to cope, Paul's grief consumed him, and he developed an unquenchable desire to end his life.

His despair led him to New York State's Mario Cuomo/Tappan Zee Bridge, which connects Westchester and Rockland counties. On that fateful night Paul chose to end it all, the high bridge shone like a beacon in the darkness, the night air eerily calm. Far below were the rocks and the rough white-capped waters of the Hudson River.

Positioning himself to jump, Paul placed one leg over the bridge railing and then another. His back to the water, he leaned out over the abyss, clinging to the railing. "Jesus, please forgive me for what I am about to do," he prayed. Then, taking a last breath, he let go.

He plummeted backward, his head leading the way toward the water as his body accelerated due to gravity's pull. Just as he felt the wind rush to envelop him, something slowed his descent. When he finally hit the water, he fell into semi-consciousness.

As he drifted downriver, a vision of the Blessed Mother appeared, and she began speaking to him in her most blessed and divine beauty. "It is not your time to leave. We have plans for you."

The vision continued throughout the night as he floated on his back in the darkness, the bridge's lights becoming fainter as he drifted farther away, his body bobbing amongst the whitecaps.

Suddenly, he felt sharp pains in his wrists. He screamed in pain and then passed out.

The next morning, he awoke on the gravel shore of the Hudson next to the train tracks. He staggered toward the tracks just as a locomotive pulling dozens of cargo cars behind it sped toward him.

The engineer pulled on his horn, thinking a drunken vagabond was about to walk in front of his speeding train and wreak havoc on his day.

Paul fell to his knees mere feet from the tracks as the cargo cars whizzed past, the wind from the train whipping his hair wildly about.

As the train receded into the distance, Paul picked himself up and staggered along the tracks until he found himself at the Tarrytown train station on the Westchester County side of the bridge. He climbed onto the platform, sending some women scurrying for the waiting train for their morning commute on the southbound side of the tracks, heading into New York.

His wounds were open and bleeding. A woman approached him and offered her shawl to cover him. He shivered and welcomed her warm kindness with a nod.

"Thank you," he said. "Can you tell me where the nearest church is?"

"I will take you there," she said.

And so, his journey into the Catholic Church began. His gifts were recognized immediately, and he was sent to the Vatican.

Paul gained a vast knowledge of Satan through his many visions. His gifts were kept secret by the highest order of the Pope and guarded by the Superior General and the secret society of the Jesuits. He was anointed to fight against evil and destroy Lucifer's plots and curses, wherever they may exist. He was given the same ranking as a cardinal, though unofficially. His ring granted him a cardinal's status and was given to him directly by the Pope to show his importance within the Church.

Paul does not allow himself any earthly pleasures or time with the devil's corrupting influences, the devil having been driven out of his body by the pure blood of Christ, which flows through his wounds of stigmata. He has put out fires for the Church all over the world. He has been summoned away from the action in the Middle East to this small Bronx neighborhood, where he was born and raised. One might ask, "What could be more important than his Middle East mission, where Christians are being beheaded and slaughtered by the hundreds?" But Paul knows his mission has enormous implications, possibly on a cataclysmic scale. The devil's work there is to placate and deceive the Pope, the Superior General, and, ultimately, Paul. Paul knows there is much more there for the devil than normal humans can comprehend.

After an all-night battle in Iraq, fighting alongside Kurdish soldiers and doing the work he was chosen to do, Paul closed his eyes to rest in the bombed-out shell of a home. He fell quickly into a deep but uneasy sleep.

As he slept, he dreamed of a sinister plot that was created by the Prince of Darkness and saw an ungodly vision he had never seen or experienced before. The fear he felt through the vision woke him up in a horrific and unsettled state. A sense of urgency prompted him to call the Superior General.

Francisco Libatore's birthplace is Naples, Italy. The man is eighty years old, but he refuses to retire. His support amongst his Jesuit followers is too great.

When the phone by his bedside rang, he reached for his glasses, glanced at the time, and then picked up the phone. "*Hola*, Hello, *Pronto?*" he says, offering a greeting in three of the seven languages he speaks.

"Please excuse me for calling you so late, Superior General," Paul said, "but I have seen a vision. I am being called to New York. I must leave immediately."

"It's okay, Paul," the Superior General said in a fatherly tone. "If you must go, then you must." His deep, raspy voice and Italian accent were evident in his speech. "Do you know in what parish you will need to stay?"

"Yes, in the Bronx, on one hundred and eighty-seventh street. It is called Mount Carmel."

"I will make arrangements for you there. God bless you on your mission."

"Thank you, Superior General."

So Paul's mission to the Bronx began.

17

PAUL MEETS PHILOMENA

After his confrontation with Mary, Paul hurries back to Mount Carmel Church. In the rectory, he asks Monsignor Anthony Mariano, his host, who is providing accommodation and anything else Paul needs for his mission, if he knows of a woman who often prays for a man in jail and her granddaughter to be reunited.

"Oh, yes," Mariano replies without hesitation. "Philomena Ciminetti. She is a regular here at Mount Carmel. She has experienced some very hard times."

This information is important to Paul, because the images of Philomena praying and her answered prayers play in his mind repeatedly. He feels the key to figuring out the rest of his vision and the true meaning of his mission will be revealed if he meets her.

"We must meet with her immediately," he says sternly.

"Of course, but why?" the monsignor asks, more than a little puzzled.

"Please, Monsignor, it is necessary."

The older man nods. "Of course. I will walk with you to her house."

They walk three blocks toward Fordham Road. On Cambrelling Avenue, they stop in front of a row of small two-family homes, the last one before an apartment building. The monsignor points to the house as they stand in front of the detectives' car.

Bulldog nudges his partner and nods at the priests. "Looks like Ciminetti is going to confess."

Murphy shakes his head. "Something seems off here. The one guy is high ranking."

"How do you know?" Bulldog asks.

"I studied the Church when I was in college," Murphy says. "I wasn't sure if I wanted to be a priest. I realized it wasn't for me. I just couldn't do without kids and sex, so I became a cop. Anyway, he's wearing a cardinal's ring, but he looks way too young to be one."

"Hopefully, he has special powers to stop you from talking about this Illuminati stuff," Bulldog says, laughing.

They watch as the two men walk up the steps onto Philomena's porch and ring her doorbell.

Philomena is surprised to find the two priests standing on her front porch. "Is everything okay?"

"Yes, everything is fine," the monsignor says. "We're just stopping in to say hello to one of Mount Carmel's most loyal parishioners. Paul has come all the way from Rome to say hello. I told him about you, and he was interested in meeting you."

Philomena nods, thinking all that's happening must have something to do with her prayer and the manifestation of blood. "Please, come in. I will make some coffee."

"Thank you," Paul replies politely.

As they enter her house, Paul asks Mariano if he can speak to Philomena alone. "Of course," the monsignor replies. "I will sit here on the couch."

"Thank you, Monsignor," Paul says. Then he turns to Philomena. "Can we talk in your kitchen?"

"Certainly," Philomena says. She leads him into the kitchen, sits down, and gestures for him to take a chair. "Please, sit."

As Paul complies, he stares at the blood-soaked tissues surrounded by rosary beads and candles.

Philomena is anxious to hear what the young man has to say, unable to hold her tongue. "Are you the one?" she asks.

He smiles. "I'm not really sure why I'm here. I was wondering if you could help me answer that. I know of your dilemma—with your son and your family—but is there something else I need to know? Is there anything more you can tell me?"

She glances at the blood-soaked tissues. "No, nothing, besides my family."

As she looks at Paul, she realizes there's something familiar about him. "Aren't you from this neighborhood? When did you become a priest from Rome?" Philomena begins to feel uncomfortable, thinking some neighborhood guys are playing a cruel joke on her. Her temper flares. "What are you doing here?"

In response, Paul gets up, walks over to her makeshift shrine, and lifts his sleeve, revealing his stigmata wound. He puts his hand next to the rosary and candles. The tissues begin to straighten, and the blood leaves the tissues and flows into his open wound. "Christ has heard your prayers," he says as he stares at the candles. "He is the reason I'm here."

Philomena drops to her knees and starts praying, asking God to forgive her for doubting him.

Paul takes her arm, helps her to her feet, and then guides her back to her chair. He kneels in front of her, holding her hand in his. "It's okay. If you can try to remember, it may help us a great deal."

She thinks for a moment and then shakes her head. "No, I can't think of anything else. I'm sorry."

A moment later, Johnny comes down. After looking at the two priests, he turns to his mother. "What's all the yelling about?"

"You go upstairs," she shoots back. "This is nothing you would understand."

"No, wait, please," Paul says. "Would you mind talking to me for just a moment?"

Johnny laughs. "I don't need to be saved, so, no, I won't be talking to you."

"You knew my brother," Paul says as Johnny heads back upstairs.

Johnny stops and looks back at Paul, beginning to recognize him. "Yeah, who?"

"They used to call him 'Allie Boy.'"

Johnny's mind races. Allie Boy was his best childhood friend. He loved Allie Boy. He was killed in a jewelry heist that went bad. Johnny had avenged his death by killing the inside guy who had set up the robbery and then alerted his boss that he was being robbed, causing the owner to pull out his gun and kill Allie Boy.

As he stares at Paul, Johnny sees Allie Boy's face, and he relaxes somewhat. "Okay, what do you want to talk about? I'm not going to confess. I'm not religious, so if that's it, you're wasting your time."

"No, I'm not looking for anything like that," Paul says. "If anything has happened recently that seemed unusual or strange to you in any way, it would help us. If you can think of anything—"

"Apart from the fact two priests are in my house?"

Paul smiles.

Johnny juts his chin at him, indicating his garb. "You became a priest?"

Paul nods. "Yes, that was my calling."

Unimpressed, Johnny starts back up the stairs. "No, nothing strange has happened," he says, his back to Paul. "Take care."

Still no closer to finding out what the rest of his mission is, Paul starts to bid Philomena goodbye, but she clutches his robe.

"Please, save my son!"

Paul smiles sadly at Philomena, her face riven with creases and worry lines.

"He has to want to be saved. I don't know if this will help, but please, let Johnny know this, even if he has agreed to sell his soul. It is not possible for the simple reason that it is not his to sell. His soul belongs to God, who created it. That means it's still redeemable."

He summons the monsignor and then turns back to Philomena. "Please, tell Johnny that we need to get together soon, before it's too late. The battle for his soul has begun."

Johnny, who is at the top of the stairs, listening, shakes his head. "Leave me the fuck alone!" he says under his breath.

18

THE DEVIL'S WORM

The devil has doubled his efforts to take Johnny's soul after being driven out of Mary, Philomena's friend. Satan has implanted his worm inside Johnny's head. It swims around and is never far from his subconscious, eventually finding its way into Johnny's brain. He reacts as if the incident has just happened, setting him off for revenge. Anyone unfortunate enough to have their name on that worm has serious trouble coming their way. It does not matter if an incident happened over thirty years prior. This time the unfortunate person is Nicky "Slim" Tortorella.

Nicky's problem with Johnny happened when Johnny was in jail. Nicky went to Philomena on numerous occasions and told her that Johnny had built up gambling debts in jail, and Nicky needed money from her, so he could pay Johnny's debts. If they were not paid, it would cause Johnny a lot of trouble with people in jail. Not wanting Johnny to get in any problems, Philomena readily gave Nicky the money on numerous occasions. It only stopped when Johnny found out and told her to stop giving him money. Nicky was a neighborhood con man. He has said some terrible things about Johnny. Nicky never thought Johnny would get out, and he felt safe. Now Nicky is not sleeping well, knowing Johnny is out. He has tried to mend fences with Johnny by sending him the money he took from Philomena back when Johnny first got out of jail, but Johnny rejected it.

Johnny has a desperate desire to satisfy the devil's worm, which lies deep within his brain. Its unquenchable thirst cannot be stilled till it is addressed in the only way the devil in Johnny knows.

He slips into a black raincoat. Then he dons a black fedora with a large brim that conceals his face. He places an old snub-nosed .38 revolver and a large .45-caliber automatic pistol into specially sewn pockets inside the raincoat. Then he sneaks out through the skylight in his hallway and disappears into the darkness. The police outside his house are oblivious to his excursion.

He makes his way to a bus stop on Fordham Road. He boards a bus and glances at the Bronx Botanical Gardens as the bus passes. Johnny, living just a few blocks away from the botanical gardens and the Bronx Zoo, has so many wonderful memories of growing up there. He recalls climbing the botanical gardens' fence and getting lost in its vast greenery and swimming in the Bronx River, which runs through the botanical gardens. He would come out smelling like a sewer, not knowing what unscrupulous dumpers put into the water.

Departing the bus at Westchester Avenue, he boards a New York City subway train that travels on an elevated train track. It's a short train ride to the Middletown Road Station, followed by a walk down a long flight of stairs to the street.

He peers inside the Zooks and Perrier's bar and grill on the corner of the block, Nicky's hangout. Johnny positions himself behind a pillar, one of many that hold up the elevated train tracks above Middletown Road and Westchester Avenue. He sees the last intoxicated barfly leaving. Now only Nicky and the bartender are inside. Johnny slowly walks across the street and enters.

Nicky, already on high alert, knowing Johnny is home, sees Johnny in the classic hit man's suit. Immediately, the hairs rise all over Nicky's body, and his fear of dying erupts. He puts on a fake smile, hoping Johnny is there for something other than to murder him. He puts his hand out to shake Johnny's and is barely able to mutter the words, "Hey, John, no hard feelings."

"None taken, cocksucker," Johnny replies. Then he blasts a .38-caliber bullet at him through the inside of his coat pocket, which conceals his hand and the gun.

It is just a flesh wound to Nicky's shoulder. Realizing what just happened to him, Nicky takes a step back. Johnny tries to fire again, but the gun jams. Nicky runs behind the bar, Johnny following him while still pulling the trigger on his defective gun.

Nicky reaches for a baseball bat from behind the bar. "Now what, tough guy?" He lifts the bat, hauling it back and aiming it at Johnny's head, wanting to smash Johnny's skull to pieces.

A loud bang erupts as Johnny blasts a second bullet from his large .45-caliber pistol inside his other pocket. Nicky staggers across the bar while looking at Johnny as he falls inches from him, dead. The large-caliber bullet pierced his heart.

The bartender stands behind the bar, looking at Johnny in a state of shock.

"Pour me a shot of scotch," Johnny says, pointing at a single-malt bottle. The bartender's hands shake uncontrollably as he places a shot glass on the bar. His shaking hands cause him to spill half the bottle of scotch on the bar in his attempt to aim for the shot glass.

Johnny lifts the overflowing and dripping shot glass. Tilting his head back, he presses the glass against his lips, savoring the scotch as he pours it slowly into his mouth and funnels it down his throat, feeling the burning of the fine scotch's sting. He never takes his eyes off the bartender, focusing an intense stare on him.

"I have two kids," the bartender says, hoping to reach the humanity in this cold, ruthless killer. He is just barely able to get the words out between his uncontrollable gasps and pounding heart.

Johnny nods slowly and coldly in acknowledgment as he loosens his grip on his gun, and his level of tension rapidly decreases. Placing the shot glass on the bar, he turns to leave, then suddenly turns back. The bartender lifts his hands to shield himself, expecting to be shot.

"Are we good?" Johnny asks.

The bartender shakes his head. "I never saw anything."

Johnny nods, then exits the bar and slowly starts his climb up the stairs that lead to the elevated subway station. The devil has put another claim in on Johnny's soul.

19

A Startling Vision

Not knowing what his mission is, Paul decides to concentrate on saving Johnny Ciminetti's soul until the rest of his assignment becomes apparent.

As he walks back to the rectory, unbeknownst to him, Bulldog is following him. He has left his partner alone on the stakeout. It is getting dark. Bulldog is in the alley behind the church. He sees Paul walking around on the second floor. He climbs a tree that leans on a fence and perches himself there so Paul is in full view.

Paul is in his sleeping quarters, walking around in his underpants. He lies down on his bed. The stigmata wounds are reintroduced as laser-like objects appear out of nowhere and strike Paul, causing large flashes of light with an almost blinding effect. They strike with precision into his wrists, reopening his wounds, making them even larger, undoing the human healing effects. He screams and cries in pain. When the episode is over, he lies in a semi-conscious state, as if seized by a vision.

Bulldog rushes down from his perch and runs back to his partner. He is shaken and unsure of what he just witnessed.

"What happened to you?" Murphy asks upon seeing Bulldog's troubled face.

"Give me the fucking flask!" Bulldog growls. Without another word, Murphy hands him a flat metal bottle filled with Hennessy cognac. Bulldog slugs down one swallow and then another. "I want off this fucking case," he says, wiping his mouth. "All this crazy shit that's happening with this Ciminetti, this crazy motherfucker!"

"Wow, calm down!" Murphy says. "What the fuck is going on?"

Bulldog can already feel the alcohol's calming effect. "Nothing, just forget about it!"

He lies down in the backseat and tries to forget what he saw, as if it were a bad dream. Taking another swallow of Hennessey, he closes his eyes, hoping he will sleep it off.

20

No Longer Part of the Family

Large Louis has no intention of letting Johnny get the first chance to kill him, so he plans to strike first. Seeking the guidance of the older, wiser members of his family, he secures a meeting with the wise old man and local Mafia boss, Tommaso, a.k.a. "Tomas," who goes back to the days of gangsters, like Mad Dog Cole, whom the United States government said was more loyal to organized crime than to the United States.

Though ninety-four, Tommaso pops in and sees as many of his family's soldiers as possible. He is strict with the old rules but has been going light on them lately, as times have changed. He does not order hits unless it is absolutely necessary because of the defection of so many soldiers, who turn on others within the family. He is a small, frail-looking old man with a skeletal frame that is starting to betray him. His stance and walk have changed throughout the years to avoid the pain of arthritis, which has riddled his body, giving him a distorted look and a limp. He never complains about his pain and refuses assistance when offered. His full head of gray hair is always combed neatly and parted at the side. Despite his age, his clean-shaven face and young-looking eyes give him an air of worldliness and wisdom.

Large Louis enters Tommaso's restaurant and gives the old man a traditional kiss on the cheek, a sign of respect and honor amongst Italian gangsters. Tommaso asks Large Louis if he would like something to eat. He shakes his head. Tommaso is troubled at what he sees.

"Louis, you look like you are not in the best of spirits. What's the problem?"

"It's Johnny Ciminetti."

The elderly man leans his chin on his right hand as Louis continues.

"He's causing a lot of grief and stirring up trouble, causing me to lose a lot of money, disrupting the flow."

The old man, always alert, knowing he may have to order a hit at any time, puts his index finger over his lips and motions Louis to walk outside so they can continue to speak in a secure area where no listening devices can be placed.

As the two men walk into the restaurant's parking lot, Tommaso turns to Louis. "Ciminetti . . . I have done some work with him. He is extremely good . . . intelligent. Have you tried to reason with him? Have a sit-down?"

"I don't believe that will work. I believe after the sit-down, he will seek his revenge."

"What did you do to him?" the old man asks.

"I slept with his daughter. She's a hooker for a black pimp who's with me."

Tommaso shakes his head in disapproval. "In the old days, we would have killed you for doing that. Fortunately for you, times have changed, and we are a kinder, gentler organization. What do you want from us?"

"You still have a relationship with Ciminetti. You can call him in, and I can do the hit on him."

The old man shakes his head slowly. "You caused this. You brought this on yourself by disrespecting him. He has done a lot of good things for us. He's not a rat. He spent twenty-four years in prison. Didn't say one word to save himself. Kept his mouth shut for our sake. And this is how you repay him? You have disgraced us! And now you want that kind of help from us? No! Go deal with this yourself! This conversation is not open to anyone in the family. You're on your own with this one."

Tommaso turns his back on Louis and walks back into his restaurant, leaving Louis out in the cold. Louis is not worried. Rashid and his crew will eliminate the threat. Louis will see to it personally.

21

Tommaso's Offer

It's a hot summer day. Tommaso is passing by Johnny's house when he decides to stop in.

Detective Murphy nudges Bulldog, who is sleeping. "Look at this! It's the old man."

Bulldog, having grown up in the neighborhood, knows exactly who Tommaso is; everybody does. "This is a big deal. Call it in and see if they want us to do anything," Bulldog says.

They watch the old man contort his body to get out of his car and make his way up the stairs. It's quite a testament to the old man's life and dedication to the Mafia of old.

An old priest, Father Carson happens by and offers Tommaso a hand up the stairs. The old man pauses on the second step and tips his cap at the priest. "No, thank you, Father."

The priest nods at Tommaso. "Have a blessed day, Tomas."

Tommaso looks again to see if the priest is familiar to him. He determines he is not. He wonders if he is an FBI agent posing as a priest. He would not put it past them.

He continues to the landing and rings Johnny's doorbell. Philomena answers the door. She knows Tommaso has run her neighborhood for the Mafia for many years. He has stopped by from time to time to pay his respects, to send his regards to Johnny, and to give her money for herself and for Johnny's commissary in prison.

"Hello, Tommaso. I know you want to see my Johnny. Hold on; I'll get him for you."

Johnny, who is shaving when Tommaso shows up, knows the old man may still pose a threat. He peeks outside for any type of offensive movement, but all is clear. He knows the police surveillance is a major deterrent to anyone trying to make a move on him. He determines Tommaso's appearance is a friendly call or an attempt to gather information, possibly to use against him later.

Johnny finishes shaving and wipes his face with a towel. Then he goes down to the kitchen, where Tommaso greets him with a hug and a kiss on the cheek. Johnny feels a genuine sense of happiness, warmth, and respect in the old man's greeting.

Tommaso grabs Johnny and gives him another kiss. "It's so good to see you here, out and free, before I die. You are a real man of honor with the cunningness of a wolf and the balls and the heart of a lion. Stay with me. You will have a strong position within the family. I will see to it."

"Tomas, I'm honored that you think of me like that. I just got home. I have many things to take care of. I can't make that kind of commitment yet."

Philomena serves them fresh espresso and homemade Italian cookies. Johnny invites the old man onto their backyard patio to drink their coffee.

"I have all the gambling in the Bronx—the card games, all the gambling machines, and all the bookmaking operations. I control them all for the family," Tommaso says. "I will give you a piece of it. You will become a very wealthy man and be able to provide for yourself and your family in ways you never could have imagined."

"I appreciate it, but Tomas, I have to get my own house in order first."

The old man peers into Johnny's eyes and then sets down his espresso, knowing full well what Johnny means. "We—and by 'we' I mean the family—will not move against you. The word is out. Everyone is to keep their hands off. Large Louis is not well liked. He's an embarrassment to us. He's into all the things we despise—drugs, prostitution, and now this thing with your daughter . . ." He shakes his head. "It's the last nail in his coffin. If he were to meet with a bad ending, no one would care." He winks at Johnny. "Do what you have to do. Once this is over, come to us. We will make you one with us, and you'll become very successful."

He finishes his espresso, still trying to read Johnny as he stares at him. "He's going to come at you with the blacks; you know this. It's all he's got."

Johnny downs the last of his espresso and then stares at the remains in his cup. "So be it!"

He realizes Tommaso has just given him the "all clear" to hit one of his own soldiers. Tommaso is also offering Johnny millions of dollars with the gambling rackets and to become a made member of his family with a high position. All is good. One less war Johnny will have to fight.

The old man rises to leave. He hugs Johnny. "You come with us. Your life is secure with us. Here is something for you." He hands Johnny a thick manila envelope stuffed with $100 bills.

Humbled, Johnny bows. "Thank you, Tommaso."

Outside, Tommaso hobbles down the sidewalk to his car. Bulldog and Murphy are standing outside Johnny's house. They approach him and flash their badges.

"What are you doing talking to Johnny? What's your business with him?" Bulldog asks.

Tommaso looks at the detective, whom he recognizes. "You're a neighborhood kid. Mafucci, right? Francesca and Paulo's son. I know your mom and dad, and I knew you, when you were a little boy."

"That's not going to get you any favoritism here," Bulldog replies.

"I did your mom and dad some pretty big favors," Tommaso says. "You should recuse yourself from any questions of me."

Bulldog is dumbfounded. He backs off, indicating his partner should take over.

"So, what's your business here?" Murphy asks.

"We have nothing to talk about," Tommaso says. "Are you going to arrest me?" He holds up his hands and waits for an answer. "No? Then I'm free to go. Have a nice day."

Before he gets into his car, he turns back and looks at Bulldog. "And you . . . you should be ashamed of yourself, trying to get me in trouble. Send my love to your mom and dad."

He drives away, leaving the detectives trying to understand what just happened.

22

Assassins' Remorse

The stage is set for an all-out assault. Large Louis gathers Rashid and his crew. It's a hot summer night. Rashid commissions his top two lieutenants, who are well versed in the art of killing, to take out Johnny and massacre everyone else in his house.

It's a simple plan. Both men will slip around the sides of the house looking for any unlocked doors or windows. Whichever one gains entrance first will alert the other, and then both men will enter and kill everyone inside. There can be no witnesses. All will be bludgeoned to death or stabbed with serrated hunting knives. It will be done this way rather than with guns so as not to alert the detectives outside.

Large Louis awaits the outcome some ninety miles away in the coastal New Jersey town of Point Pleasant. It's a small community with quaint restaurants and shops, a popular vacation spot on the shore that attracts thousands of tourists during the summer months. It has an early-American atmosphere, and even its residents seem mostly blonde and blue-eyed, as sweet as apple pie, folksy and homey. It's a pleasant place, just as the town's name says. But the Bronx will not be nearly as pleasant if Large Louis has his way tonight.

He is making his way all over town so as many witnesses as possible can place him there. He goes from place to place, making sure he is noticed spending money and being loud. All this is to afford him an alibi to avoid being suspected of such bloody and despicable acts of murder.

At 9:05 p.m., Rashid's lieutenants make their way toward Johnny's house, jumping over fences and sneaking through backyards. As they approach Johnny's place, two large Italian Neapolitan Mastiffs, used as watchdogs, start barking from the neighbor's yard. The assassins stop and remain crouched until the dogs quiet down.

One of the assassins is a tall black male with a prizefighter's physique. His hair is cut close to his scalp with a razor part along the side. His small features and light skin give him the appearance of being interracial. He scales a tall cement wall that divides Johnny's yard from the neighbor's, lifting his massive body with just one hand.

The second assailant has a tougher time getting over the wall. He gets up on the wall and lies horizontally on top of it before he flips off the wall and lands in a garden of tomatoes, parsley, and zucchini, crushing the plants, which break his fall.

He rises. He is a tall man, six feet three inches of massive flesh. He has huge shoulders and a large gut, but he has a lot of muscle under his fat. He wears his hair in a medium-sized Afro. His skin is dark, and his large, flat nose, large lips, and massive hands make him a scary figure.

Little do the assassins realize the dogs' barking has served as an alarm for Johnny. He watches them from his roof as they split up and move around the sides of his house, trying the doors and windows.

Johnny has made something he calls a "body-snatching machine." It allows him to strap himself in and, with the help of a large swivel arm, lower himself down, retrieve a heavy weight, and bring his prey back up to the roof. It is made with weights and car tire rims, and it is most effective.

Johnny follows the would-be killer with the big Afro. He swoops down with a large hunting knife, sticking it into the man's spine at the back of his neck, severing his c6 and c5 vertebra, cutting his nerves, and severing his airway. The man's large body goes limp. Johnny wraps a thick leather barber strap around his victim and then, like a spider cocooning an unfortunate fly caught in his web, pulls hard on another leather strap and is lifted back up to the roof with his dying catch.

The large man gurgles and gasps for air as Johnny lays him down in the center of his roof, swinging the arm of his body-snatching machine over to the other side of the building.

Staring at his light-skinned would-be killer, who is prying open a window, Johnny swoops down again and lands directly behind his kill. He plunges his knife into the man's lower vertebra, just below his usual mark on the neck but still rendering his assailant helpless. The man's legs collapse as he goes limp. His nerves are severed by the second strike in his spine, which also cuts off his air circulation, rendering him helpless.

Johnny lifts the man back up to his roof. Then he plunges his knife deep into the man's back. Johnny grinds his teeth in anger as he faces his dying prey. "You wanted to kill me, you cocksucker!"

He tosses the man next to his dying friend. "What did you accomplish here? I hope you both learned a very valuable lesson." He lectures them like a professor talking to his class. "And what would that be? Come on, tell me, please, tell me that you learned something. Well, I'll tell you, you black motherfuckers, when it comes to killing, some people are just much better at this kind of shit."

Looking at their bodies as they lay on the cold tar roof, he realizes both men have expired. He stops his taunts and lowers their bodies down to a side door that leads to his basement. Then he drags them inside and places them next to a large band saw. It has a long thin blade with a razor-sharp edge that spins extremely fast. It's made for cutting cow and pig carcasses, the same as you would find in a butcher shop. He also has an open shower in his basement, inside of which he has placed large meat hooks.

After slitting their throats and plunging a large hunting knife into their hearts, he hangs the bodies upside-down to bleed out. He washes all the blood from his victims and hoses it toward the drain. When the victims are finished bleeding out, he cleans all traces of blood with bleach.

Then he puts on his butcher coat and pulls out some sharp butcher knives and hits "play" on his old eight-track player and starts playing Italian music by his favorite Italian singer, Jimmy Roselli. He turns up the volume and then begins to slice the first body. The music is to hide the sound of the band saw cutting through flesh and bone.

As body parts are dismembered, they fall from the band saw into a large, gray, plastic trunk. The remaining blood runs into the drain that leads into the open shower. He continues running the body parts into the band saw, cutting them small enough so his neighbor's Italian bull mastiffs can eat them. He gained his butchering skills by way of his first and only job as a young teenager. He worked in the neighborhood butcher shop before he went into a life of crime and murder.

When he is finished, he hoses the tile floor and sweeps the rest of the blood into the shower drain. He places the victims' heads into his basement refrigerator, thinking they'll come in handy later.

Back in Point Pleasant, about two hours after the attack, Large Louis calls Rashid for an update.

"What happened?"

"I don't know," Rashid says, sounding unsure.

"You don't know? What do you mean you don't know?"

"I don't know!" Rashid replies, irritated. "They haven't gotten back to me yet."

Louis is stunned. He feels a sinking sensation in his stomach. He knows what this means. "Forget it; they're dead," he mutters. "Johnny got 'em."

Rashid laughs. "Those are some serious dudes. That little man is not going to get them. They'll get *him!*"

Louis is unable to think clearly, thoughts rushing through his head. "They're dead!" he shouts and then hangs up. He hurries to his car and rushes back to the Bronx to retrieve his son.

Two and a half hours later, Frankie, who is on an all-night cocaine binge, is feeling full of false courage. After Rashid fills him in on recent events, he smacks the table. "Fuck this!" He looks at another up--and-coming gangster, Tony the Geep. He's the same age as Frankie and part of his crew. "Let's contact this motherfucker and meet with him."

They retrieve Philomena's phone number and make a call. Even though it's 4 a.m., Johnny picks up, but he doesn't say anything, just listens.

"Meet me at the all-night grocery on one hundred and eighty-seventh and Hoffman," Frankie says. "Let's talk." Then he hangs up.

As he walks out of Rashid's building with Tony the Geep, he punches the air and dances around like a boxer. "Let's do this! I know this motherfucker isn't going to show. I'll show him!"

He walks up 187th Street, the main street toward Hoffman Street. They look around and see no one. Frankie smirks. "Told you he wouldn't show."

Just then, Johnny emerges from the store and approaches them. He stops and smiles. "I got something for you and one for you."

He hands each of them a paper shopping bag. Frankie looks into his bag and is gripped with fear, causing him to lose control of his bladder. Inside is one of the heads of the would-be hit men. Urine pours down his right pant leg, drenching his shoe and forming a puddle around it. As he continues to shake in fear, a moist brown stain forms on the seat of his pants. He has lost all control of his bodily functions.

Johnny smiles and nods.

Tony the Geep is also frozen in fear. His choice of drug is angel dust, and he is under the influence of the hallucinogenic substance. He sees the man with the Afro staring up at him from the bottom of the bag. Then the man's head starts talking to him. "Hey, man, don't fuck with this motherfucker. Look what he did to me. I should have never listened to Rashid and came out here tonight. Damn, man."

Johnny is still staring at both men with the distant glare of a lunatic.

The scene is broken when a car screeches around the block. Inside is Large Louis. Rashid informed Louis of his son's meeting with Johnny.

He opens the passenger door as he jams his brakes. "Get in the car!" He grips a pistol, keeping it trained on Johnny. "Keep away from my son, you crazy motherfuckin' nut!"

Johnny turns his sadistic smile toward Large Louis. A surreal feeling of fear fills Louis. Just the look on Johnny's face is all it takes to know what he's dealing with. He's sure he's looking at the face of pure evil, embedded deep in Johnny's soul.

Frankie and Tony the Geep jump into the car. Then Louis puts the car in reverse, guns the gas, and burns rubber as his car whips around, facing away from Johnny. Large Louis's wheels catch the pavement, and they speed off, leaving behind a cloud of smoke.

Johnny returns to the comfort of his home, plotting to snuff out the only thing that stands between him and his beloved daughter.

23

A Shocking Confession

Sunday morning services are being held at Mount Carmel Church. With mass over, Father Carson, a tall, elderly Irish man with a thin frame and thinning hairline, is about to leave the rectory to hear confession. He has a welcoming smile that gives him the look of a trusting grandfather, but his gait seems labored.

Paul walks past and then stops, a look of concern on his face. "Father, are you feeling well?"

Father Carson forces a grin. "Yes, just a bit tired," he says, his voice weak. "I've had to do so many masses and hear so many confessions this week, filling in for Monsignor. He's been so busy with all his extra chores."

Father Carson sticks his finger into his clerical collar to separate his clothing from his skin, trying to get air between his body and his garment to help him cool down. Paul knows his visit has put a strain on the priest's parish duties. It has been hard for the entire staff.

"Would you mind if I heard confessions today?" Paul asks.

Father Carson looks up to the heavens, takes a deep breath, and then exhales. He relaxes his shoulders and looks at Paul, smiling in relief. "Would you? I mean, can you?"

"Of course. You need to rest. Please, I'll be fine. Just go up to your room and rest."

Father Carson thanks him and heads upstairs to his bedroom for a much-needed nap as Paul dresses himself in a traditional stole to hear confessions from the regular Sunday parishioners.

As he enters the main part of the church, a tall blonde woman in her early thirties stares at him. Paul can feel her eyes. He turns toward her, and it takes only a second for realization to settle in.

Oh no, it's her! It's her! his thoughts cry out. His mind races over what he has just seen, clamoring through his body. Dormant emotions from a past time ignite and collide inside him. His heartbeat and pulse rate accelerate. Throbbing blood flows through his veins with intermittent rhythm.

His knees feel weak. His throat tightens and dries as he forces himself to swallow. He turns toward the confessional, pulls the door open, steps inside, and closes the door behind him. He breaks into prayer to prepare himself to hear confession. Once he composes himself, he feels he is ready to begin.

He slides open a small door that exposes a screen, showing a dimly lit silhouette of his confessor's face. A woman.

"Hello, Paul," she says uncertainly in an unmistakable voice he has heard in his head thousands of times over the years. "Lisa told me she saw you around the neighborhood and that now you're a priest. Is that where you went when you left?"

"Do you have anything to confess?" Paul replies sternly, ignoring her question.

"Yes. I love you, and I'm sorry for the way things turned out."

Paul struggles to maintain his composure. "We are talking about your sins. Do you have any?"

"I've made mistakes," she replies, her voice cracking. "I never should have left you. I think about you so often. I want to run away with you."

"You had your chance, and you chose another," Paul snaps.

"You know I was forced to," she says through her tears. "My father threatened to cut me off from my family, and he got so ill over us being together, he almost died."

"I can't do this with you now," Paul says, his voice strained, irritated.

"I want to see you," she says, fighting to control her emotions. "There is so much more—"

"That's enough. I'm a priest now, and you are married. It's over."

She shakes her head, "My husband died of pancreatic cancer this spring."

Why is she telling me this? Does she think this is going to make all that happened right? How can I feel indifferent about a tragedy in someone's life? Remember, you're a priest.

He snaps away from his thoughts. "I'm sorry to hear that," Paul replies, "but please, you must go."

She shakes her head, refusing to accept Paul's answer. "I need this, Paul, please!"

Feeling his emotions tugging at him, he does his best to remain stern. "I have an entire congregation to hear confessions from. Not now!"

"When?" she asks, her face wet with tears.

"I don't know."

"I've waited so long to say these things to you. I can't let you go without you hearing them."

Paul struggles to avoid surrendering to the only love he has ever wanted. "Please, don't make this any harder on either of us. You must leave."

She shakes her head again but stands up slowly. "I must speak with you," she says as she exits the confessional.

Paul has a tough time remaining focused as he listens to the rest of the confessions. Hours later, as he exits the booth, a voice calls to him. "Paul, please wait!" He turns to see Rita stand up from the wooden pew directly across the narrow aisle from the confessional.

"Can't you see?" he asks. "There's nothing more to do here. Time and events have shaped our lives, and now they divide us forever. Continue with your life."

He turns and heads for the rear exit, but she follows. "You know you don't mean that."

"You must stop this," Paul says, still walking. "Release yourself from this part of your past."

She walks faster to catch up with him. "You love me, and I love you. It was supposed to be us who married. I was young and foolish. I felt alone. I didn't know what else to do. Paul, please forgive me!"

Paul stops to face her. He gazes into her big, deep-blue eyes, her pale skin and beautiful face. It is all so alluring and intoxicating. All his deeply stored feelings start to reemerge. He feels himself weaken, and he can tell she senses it. Paul has lusted for her so many times.

"No, this is wrong!" he shouts and then breaks away and walks at a faster pace.

He hurries to the rectory, goes inside, and shuts the door behind him, feeling safe now that he is tucked away within its confines.

He sits in his room, clasping his hands and leaning his head on them. The phone rings. It's the front desk, staffed by Mrs. Arceola, a local grandmother who volunteers her time at Mount Carmel.

"Father Paul, there's a woman here who seeks counseling with you," she says with a slight Bronx Italian-American accent. "She seems to be having a tough time, poor thing."

He remains silent.

"Father Paul, are you still there?" she asks, concerned.

His first thoughts are to just send her away. Then he decides it's better to face her now and put an end to it forever. "Yes, I'll be right there."

He rises from his chair, lets out a sigh of dread, and walks toward the front of the rectory.

Rita is the love of his life, the one he will never forget for the rest of his days. She has always lingered in his mind. Her lips were filled with so much passion. Her large blue eyes are accentuated by her pale skin, and her perfectly straight white teeth blended so perfectly with her fine features that she looks more Swedish than Italian. Her blonde hair and light eyes are prevalent in her parents' homeland of Bari, Italy. Her long, lean athletic body carries her perfectly shaped female physique, which is flawless, like an athlete. Long, attractive, shapely legs prop up her five-foot-ten frame. Her beauty is meant for the runways of the world, but she is a local neighborhood girl from the Bronx. Born into a traditional Italian immigrant family, having children and raising a family are her sole aspirations.

Paul came into her life when he was a young buck. She already had a boyfriend, locked into a lackluster relationship with a boy whom her father had chosen for her. Her father felt he could control the boy and that she would still love, respect, and fear her father rather than her husband. Her desire for freedom from her home and her controlling father was the reason for continuing her monotonous relationship with her boyfriend.

Paul and his older brother, Allie Boy, were tough neighborhood kids with bad reputations who hung with the street crowd. Her attraction to Paul was immediate.

One morning on her way to the local Catholic high school for girls, she noticed Paul and some friends hanging out in front of an all-night cab company across the street from her house. He had been out all night. It was so alluring and exciting to her, the street life. Paul's movie star looks resembled Elvis, her idol. She had heard of his reputation as a tough ex-boxer with rough nights out in the clubs of Westchester County and the Bronx, so she set her sights on him and showed up in places where she knew he would be.

One night, Paul, making money as a bouncer, was standing at the front door of a club, when Rita appeared. She was only seventeen and had just gotten her driver's license. She had snuck out with her father's car while he was sleeping.

"What are you doing here?" Paul asked.

She shrugged, looking as innocent as ever. She wore tight, light-blue jeans that showed off her amazing physical attributes and a tight pale-yellow top that fit snugly around her growing breasts. She was a fresh, blooming flower. He asked her to come in, but she refused, choosing to stand with him by the door and talk.

Paul and Rita agreed to meet secretly on a quiet side street just across from their neighborhood. It was referred to as "the country," and it was just on the north side of Fordham Road near 191st Street in front of Fordham University. A quiet setting in the middle of the Bronx, it looked more like the country than a Bronx street. It was also safe. No one would notice them meeting there.

It was a rainy day, and Paul was late. He hurried to "the spot," as they came to know it. Not even sure if she would be there, he turned the corner, and there she was, holding an umbrella as she waited in the rain. He pulled over and opened his car's passenger door. She smiled as she got in.

He traveled up to Westchester near a family-owned bagel store and parked behind the shopping center, where they talked for a while. Then Paul pulled her close and put his lips on hers.

He kissed me! she thought, causing a release of energy, generated by a long and much desired moment. Little did she know that kiss would put her on the path to the most passion she could ever imagine, a physical attraction that would be embedded in her for the rest of her life.

This is going to be amazing! she thought, and she was right. Never would she feel such passion, such raging hormones, and such deep desires ignited and then satisfied over and over again.

Paul was amazed at how such an innocent-looking young girl could stay with him and continue to want more. She was his ultimate partner and turn on. They had an undeniable chemistry, like a nuclear blast. Extreme passion was unleashed that would stay with them forever, replaying repeatedly in their minds. For them to deny it would be impossible.

When Rita's father found out about her and Paul, he made her abandon him. She has lived with so much regret that she did not fight for what she knew to be her true love. Her mother, trying to keep her family together, told Rita she would forget about Paul and convinced her to go back to her boyfriend. Rita believed her mother at first, but her passion stayed with her no matter how hard she tried to dismiss it.

She longs for that feeling of being in love. She wants to feel alive and experience that feeling of wild, raging passion. It is the most intense physical and emotional feeling she has ever known. Her unquenchable desire for Paul still knows no boundaries.

There is real danger if they are alone together. Paul knows the weakness he still harbors for her, the deep scars he bears. The challenge is to stay strong, knowing he is married to the Church.

Is God testing me? he wonders. *Oh, Lord, please give me strength to resist this temptation and the weakness of the flesh.*

Paul opens the door and walks into a simple office tucked behind a small maze of walls in the back of the rectory. It is a medium-sized room with an old maple desk and two wooden chairs stained the same color as the desk. The office is dimly lit by a low-voltage wooden lamp that matches the maple furniture.

Paul pushes the button of an antiquated intercom system that connects to the front desk. "Please, send her in."

He sits behind the desk, his last resort of protection. Rita enters, still in a disheveled state. He stands and motions for her to sit in one of the chairs in front of the desk.

As Mrs. Arceola closes the door behind Rita, Paul feels the danger level heighten. He feels uneasy, helpless in confronting the face of his weakness.

"What good is this conversation going to do for either one of us?" he asks as Rita sobs.

Rita regains her composure, wiping her eyes with a tissue. "I need to tell you so many things."

Paul closes his eyes, rocking his head back and forth. "If you think this will help you, then go ahead, do it."

Rita clears her throat. "I was so young, foolish, and immature. I enjoyed all the attention that was lavished on me by you, my father, and him. I never meant to hurt you. As soon as you stopped coming around, I realized you were the one that I loved. I couldn't stop thinking about you. I spend all my free time thinking, what if I would have done this different or done that different? I shouldn't have been so stupid. I want you back in my life forever."

Paul feels he must finally ask the question he has pondered so many times. "If you found true and genuine love, how can you leave so easily?"

"I never stopped loving you," she replies without hesitation. "It has only grown stronger. I never would have gone through with the marriage if you had stayed around, but you left, and no one knew where you were. I was so lonely because of my love for you. I still am."

Paul nods, Rita having finally voiced the words he has longed so desperately to hear.

Rita is still sobbing. Paul gets up and puts his hand on her shoulder to comfort her. She stares intensely into his eyes, her look telling him she hopes his love for her is still there.

Finally, she stands up, nudges her way between his arms, and leans her body on his, resting her head in his shoulder. Then she lifts her head up. With her hand, she reaches for his chin, straightens his head, and pulls his face down to hers. He resists, pushing her away, but his fight is short-lived. She lays her lips on his, and the whirling feeling of euphoria smashes within his brain, destroying any remaining resistance. As she parts her lips, the passion that has been denied for so many years is unleashed once again.

24

THE NEW MOVEMENT

The Superior General, Francisco Libatore, is tucked inside the walls of the Curia Generalizia in Rome, the world headquarters of the Jesuit Order. Francisco is in his own conclave. His pristine offices and sleeping quarters are on the premises. The walls and floors look as if every stone has just been placed. His inner sanctum is well below the structure of the Curia Generalizia. It stretches through mazes of twisting tunnels with dimly lit stairwells that lead to different chambers, resembling a medieval castle. Francisco feels comfortable in his skin there. His surroundings truly fit his makeup.

This is where the work of the Superior General, the Black Pope, is done. He knows every space, every nook and cranny, and has handpicked all who work there. He affectionately calls his offices "the dungeons." He walks around in a black friar's robe and leather sandals. He is a true general, who has honed his craft and his skills, which are now absolute. His offices look like that of any large country's state department or military headquarters, with maps of all parts of the globe displayed on the walls and laid out on tables. The maps have red pins stuck in them, depicting where his work is being done in the world.

Francisco heads up the Roman Catholic Church's equivalent to the United States' CIA or Russia's old KGB. Conspiracy theorists throughout the world claim his operations are responsible for everything from the overthrow of governments to the assassination of John F. Kennedy and the death of Pope John Paul I. None of this is proven, and in each case, none of the rumors are true. Nevertheless, haters of the Church and the Superior General's work continue to spread lies about him and the Catholic Church throughout the world.

To say the Church does nothing it is accused of doing to further its agenda is naive. Any religious organization whose teachings are different from the other major religions must readjust and evolve continually, protecting itself to ensure its survival, or it will surely perish.

Morning comes early for Francisco. At 4:30 a.m., as he takes his shower, he has a feeling something is going to be different about this day.

While drying himself, he looks in the mirror and sees a stranger's face behind him. He turns around, but no one is there. He looks back in the mirror again and sees nothing but his own reflection. Shrugging it off, he finishes getting ready for the day. After slipping into his comfortable monk's robe and stepping into his sandals, he walks into his kitchen and finds a freshly made espresso sitting on his table, brought by one of his aides.

After breakfast, he walks through "the dungeons" to his spacious office, which is filled with large hand-carved marble sculptures of various religious figures. The office's floors and walls are made with lavish vein-free Carrara Italian marble, brought from the finest marble quarries in Carrara, Lunigiana, Italy. The ceiling is a brilliant tile mosaic of the resurrection of Christ. The marble walls are decorated with religious paintings by the world's best-known artists, some of the works worth millions of dollars. He often hosts dignitaries from all over the world. Frequently, they stare in amazement at his extensive art collection. He often jokes, "After all, there have to be some advantages that come with this job."

He turns on his office light and is startled to find a young man sitting in front of his desk, the same man whose face he saw earlier in his bathroom mirror. The young man has boyish looks and a thick head of black hair with a recent and meticulous haircut. His manicured fingernails and freshly shaved face made him look even younger than his thirty-two years. His large sunken eyes and long thin nose above his thin lips give him the appearance of a sophisticated elitist. It's clear from his expression that no matter where he is, he thinks he is much smarter than anyone else in the room.

He has a thin, wiry frame. He is wearing a long black cassock robe with a red sash belt, topped off with a white priest's collar. His robe is impeccably clean and pressed, and the room is filled with the aroma of his expensive European cologne.

"What are you doing here?" Francisco asks. "How did you get through security?"

"I am here on behalf of the New Movement in the Church," the young man replies, "and on behalf of Cardinal Angelo Martino."

Francisco realizes who the young man is. He has heard much of him. He is Alphonso Procaccino, leader of the so-called New Movement. He is a rising young star within the Catholic Church, and he works for Cardinal Angelo Martino, dean of the cardinals for the Holy See of Rome.

Alphonso is Cardinal Martino's personal liaison to the New Movement. Alphonso's position was a gesture of peace through weakness. The old traditional conservatives have lost a lot of ground, and much power has shifted to the New Movement. The conservatives thought it would be wiser to share power in the Church to stop a political uprising that may cause irreparable damage to their position, but they were mistaken.

The New Movement's agenda is to have an active role in the Church's policy of tolerance and inclusion and to have the Church recognize and welcome gays and people of other sexual orientations into the fold. Not only do they want the Church to accept such people, they want the Church to affirm that they are living a different but normal way of life.

The conservatives think this initiative is too bold, and it will never get the support of traditional Catholics. It will cause an uproar throughout the world that can be neither silenced nor contained, but they find themselves at an impasse.

Mere consideration of such a proposal would have been unheard of in the past. However, the Church is finding it difficult to attract decent and skilled people from the mainstream of Catholic followers due to the Church's requirement of celibacy for priests and the recent sexual scandals that have rocked the Church to its core. Unable to draw from the mainstream, there is no way to replenish the Church's conservative core. It has become a progressively liberal institution, made up of liberal elitists, who will soon be dictating Church doctrine and policy to its clergy and the masses.

The conservatives are dwindling and losing power and authority. It is like an older lion hiding behind his roar to hold off a pack of hungry hyenas that sense his age and weakness, knowing his time has come. Once the Church accepts the New Movement's agenda, the group's last demand is for the old guard to relent on many of its core beliefs or face certain mutiny and possibly a loss of all power. So, their concession is a way to retain power and remain at the top of the Church's hierarchy for a little while longer.

Alphonso is young, but he's a shrewd manipulator and a con artist. His dark Hollywood tan and feminine mannerisms invoke disdain within Francisco, as does his lisp, which snaps at the air as his words leave his mouth.

"One of our main goals is to close down your medieval tunnels and offices. In certain instances, your work has given the Church a bad name."

Francisco smirks as he looks at the man's fresh robe and designer shoes. *Fifteen hundred US dollars or more*, he thinks. He is not about to surrender easily. "So, my young brother in Christ, you come here without being noticed or invited. Unannounced, you show up here in my office. Impressive." He reaches for a tangerine and begins peeling it. "Nobody before you has ever done something so bold—or so disrespectful." He leans forward, as if to tell a secret. "Because it is just not allowed," he whispers through a seething grin.

Alphonso swipes his hand at the air to show he will not be intimidated. "I am here on behalf of Cardinal Angelo Martino. We are not going to do things the old way anymore. We are a new and more inclusive church. Your way of doing business here is no longer required, nor will it be tolerated."

Francisco bows his head, as if cowering before Alfonso. "Forgive me. I did not know the Pope had died and you had been elected as the new head of the Church. Please, forgive me, Your Eminence."

Francisco's ultraconservative beliefs in the old world's order has caused him to bump heads with the New Movement on many occasions. He has fought hard political battles against the New Movement and won most, if not all, of them. He has a true contempt for their agenda. He feels it will erode, corrode, and, ultimately, destroy the Church.

His commitment to Christ's teachings has always been the center of his and the Church's doctrine and direction throughout the centuries. He feels Christ left instructions on how he wanted his Church to function. He feels nothing but contempt for the young priest and his New Movement. Now he is in Francisco's office with so much power, given to him by Cardinal Martino.

"So, you are going to close down our operations, and by whose orders are you demanding this, my young brother? Did Angelo send you to do this?"

The young priest shoots up out of his chair. "It's over, old man! Our movement is taking over the Church, and you will be one of its casualties."

Francisco's deep resentment for Alphonso reaches the boiling point. Filled with rage, he stands and points his index finger at the young priest's face. "You are not the New Movement of anything! You and your group are a cancer in the body of Christ. You are what one of the great popes warned us about, the smoke of Satan that has entered the Church!" He points to the door of his large office. "Get out of here, and don't come back! You will not disgrace this sacred ground with your presence again."

Francisco turns toward the door. "Manny, come!" In his anger, Francisco does not realize that Manny, his most trusted advisor and closest friend, is already in the room, alerted by Francisco's yelling.

Seeing Manny, Francisco refocuses his eyes on Alphonso. "Get him out of here! I don't want to see his face here ever again. I don't care how you do it; throw him out if he resists."

Manny is an expert in Brazilian Jiu-Jitsu and a former boxer. Growing up in a poor, tough neighborhood in Rio de Janeiro's inner city made him hard as nails. He received his calling to be a priest late in life and was quickly recruited for the Superior General's work. His nose is slightly flattened from his boxing days and is prevalent on his rugged face. He still retains his boxer build through intense workouts and martial arts training. He is a heavyweight, his tall frame and muscular body menacing even beneath his monk's robe.

Alphonso sneers at Manny and then looks at Francisco. "I'm leaving for the Pope's office now."

"I said for you to get out of here now, or you will never leave this place."

As Manny moves toward the young upstart, Alphonso turns toward the office door, his robe billowing up from his feet. As he whisks himself away, his new Italian shoes echo loudly throughout the chamber as they tap against the marble floor.

25

An Unfortunate Incident

An emissary from the Pope summons Francisco to a meeting concerning his recent confrontation with Alphonso. The messenger also says the Holy Father will make a final decision about the future of Francisco's operations. The meeting is scheduled in three days.

Satan has bogged down Francisco and distracted Paul from his mission. Now the New Movement threatens to topple the Catholic Church from within through Alphonso Procaccino, Satan's man on the inside.

Francisco summons Manny to his office and gestures for him to sit, which Manny does with the obedience of a robot. "Manny, I want you to follow Alphonso. See where he goes, what he does. Find out what you can, and then come straight back to me."

He looks around his office, and, for the first time, feels he might lose it all. He turns back to Manny. "I'm going to need the information for my meeting with the Holy Father and Cardinal Martino."

Manny nods and bows his head. "Yes, Your Eminence."

He leaves immediately and tracks Alphonso to a cocktail party. He is with a younger man who remains close by him at all times.

Later, Manny follows the young priest to his apartment in Rome, where he changes into casual wear, dressed for summer. He is with the same young man he was with at the cocktail party. They get onto a Vespa scooter and ride through the streets of Rome, stopping in cafés, enjoying food and drinks and, at times, holding hands and kissing.

Manny reports back to the Superior General immediately. Francisco determines that Alphonso is unholy and an enemy of the Church. Acting on his lust with another man has condemned him as an agent of Satan, and he must be dealt with before he harms the Church any further.

The meeting with the Pope and Cardinal Angelo Martino is scheduled for the next morning, with Francisco's position, power and the future of his operations in the Church in total jeopardy. Francisco dispatches Manny and two other priests, who are experts in espionage and counter-espionage and who are also trained assassins. Manny is given instructions on how to handle the operations concerning Alphonso in detail by the Superior General.

The early morning meeting with the Pope, the Superior General, and Cardinal Angelo Martino begins in a Vatican courtroom. The pure white marble floor flows across the large auditorium and continues up the steps that lead to the head of the room and onto a large platform. Two large columns of red-veined marble stand on either side of the platform. Vases filled with fresh floral arrangements add brilliance and color to the massive chamber.

A large throne where the Pope will sit is situated between the two massive marble columns that reach up to the high ceiling over the platform. The ceiling above the platform is made of a vivid stained-glass portrait that depicts Jesus standing in front of Pontius Pilate. The Latin words inscribed into the bottom of the image say, "Judge others as you would have them judge onto you." The rest of the ceiling is vaulted in gold-leafed frames that surround hand-painted portraits of angelic figures fitted into each of the frames with vibrant clarity and astonishing colors. The paintings were painted in the 1800s and have just been restored to their original brilliance.

Wallpaper made of thick deep-red and white material intertwines into an inlay of hand-laid floral patterns on the massive walls, which seem to go on forever. Various pieces of art hang on the walls, including large sculptures of religious figures made from marble and clay. Two long granite tables stretch in front of the elevated platform. The breathtaking room creates unique and surreal feelings of extravagance and importance. Large hand-carved chairs sit behind the long tables. The Pope takes his place on the platform. He looks over the room and the tables, which are directly in front of him.

Cardinal Martino sits at one of the tables in front of the platform. Beside him are two young priests with law degrees. They represent the New Movement, and they are fully prepared and eager to present their case for ending the Superior General's reign. Cardinal Martino is in agreement with the New Movement's efforts to retire Francisco and his operations once and for all.

On the other table, the Superior General is sitting with two older Jesuit priests, who are biblical scholars and experts in canon law. They are familiar with church procedures, protocol, and doctrine. They will argue in favor of keeping the Superior General and his operations going and demonstrate his importance to the Church.

Cardinal Martino is anxious to begin, but Alphonso has not yet appeared, delaying the proceedings. Just then, a brisk wind of excitement enters the chamber as copies of Rome's leading newspaper, *la Repubblica*, are whisked into the chamber by two of the Pope's aides. The papers are distributed quickly to the Pope, Cardinal Martino, and the Superior General. The front-page headline reads, "Priest with ties to the Vatican killed in murder-suicide." Beneath it is a picture of Alphonso.

The Holy Father lifts his head from the paper and stares at Francisco in astonishment. Cardinal Martino is also dumfounded, casting an accusing glare at Francisco. The Superior General feels both men's deeply concentrated stares, but he tries his best to ignore them.

Manny enters the chamber and hurries to sit down next to Francisco. This is the first time the Superior General has seen Manny since he was sent on his mission to deal with Alphonso. "Manny, was it necessary to do what you did?" Francisco whispers. "He was supposed to be detained, so he would not be at this meeting, and we could have more time."

"Father General, we did not do it," Manny whispers back. "It was done before we arrived. Both men were dead."

The Father General places his hand on his chin as he leans his ear closer to Manny, closing his eyes in concentration.

"It is true what the papers are saying," Manny continues. "It was a murder-suicide. We did not do it. It was a lover's triangle. His lover found him with another man and killed him. Then he turned the gun on himself."

Emboldened, Francisco's eyes shoot open as he stares daggers at Cardinal Martino. He stands, so everyone in the chamber can see and hear him. "Angelo, why do you stare at me with such contempt and accusation? I have no involvement in this heinous act that claimed the life of young Alphonso. He died at the hands of a jealous lover."

Cardinal Martino, embarrassed at the insinuation in front of the Pope, shakes his head as he tries to return the emphasis to Francisco. He removes his glasses before speaking. "Superior General, if only your reputation did not precede you into this chamber. Then your denial would not seem so ludicrous or implausible."

"Francisco," the Pope intervenes sternly. He opens his hand and motions Francisco to come to the front of the altar. Francisco complies and stands before him. The Pope points to the heavens, as if to coerce a confession: "In front of our Holy God, tell of your involvement with Alphonso's death."

Francisco spreads his arms in front of him, his palms facing up, as if he were in prayer, and looks up to the heavens. "I swear this to my living God and Savior, my hands are clean of any involvement, as are those of any who are associated with me. We had nothing to do with Alphonso Procaccino's death. May Almighty God have mercy and pity on his soul."

The Pope looks at Cardinal Martino, who gives the Pope a reluctant nod of approval, though his face is filled with skepticism and disgust. The Pope is satisfied and ends the proceedings. The Superior General and his operations will live on.

Powerful forces inside the New Movement question the legitimacy of the murder-suicide. However, the death of the New Movement's leader puts the conservatives firmly back in control for at least the next several years. The New Movement cannot recover quickly from the loss of such a shrewd, charismatic leader.

Whispers that Francisco ordered the murders echo throughout the Vatican. For the Superior General, the Black Pope, it is just another day at work.

Now able to concentrate on Paul and his mission, he calls Mount Carmel Church. "Hello, Monsignor Mariano. I have not been able to get in touch with Paul for the past few days. Can you connect me with him?"

"No, I don't know where he is, Superior General."

"What do you mean?"

"He has vanished and taken a female parishioner with him. We are unable to reach him. The woman's father and family are here right now, and they are very upset. This is becoming a scandal for us."

Francisco is stunned by the news. "I'm coming there with three others. Have things ready for us."

"Yes, Your Excellency. It will be such an honor to have you visit us here at Mount Carmel."

26

Unexpected Visitors

A knock on the rectory door at 3 a.m. awakens Monsignor Mariano. Thinking it must be some teenagers playing a prank, he rolls out of bed and goes down to the rectory's front door.

"Who is it?"

"We are here from Rome," a voice replies.

Monsignor Mariano opens the door and is shocked to find the Superior General and his companions on his doorstep. He bows before Francisco, kissing his ring.

A few nuns, startled awake by the noise, also appear at the door. When they see the Superior General, one the most respected leaders of the Church, they also bow down and kiss his ring.

"Please, go back to sleep," Francisco says to the nuns. "I am sorry for getting in so late. It is just that this is such an urgent matter facing your church that it requires my personal attention."

The nuns know of the scandal brewing with Paul and Rita. They feel the problem will be dealt with in a more serious manner now that representatives from the Vatican are there, but a thought lingers in their minds: Why can't the local New York cardinal handle this? Why has Rome gotten involved?

The rectory is crowded with the Superior General, his three companions, the monsignor, and the three nuns. Francisco asks Mariano if he can show them to their quarters.

"Yes, of course, Superior General. I'm afraid there are only two bedrooms available."

Francisco smiles. "Do not worry. We will sleep two to a room."

Mariano bows. "Oh, that solves so many problems, Your Eminence."

At the crack of dawn, Francisco is up pacing in the rectory, thinking. He is greeted by one of the nuns, who has made him coffee and gives him a Stella D'oro, a sweet Italian cookie, as she starts breakfast for everyone.

Two hours later, they are eating at the rectory's dinner table. It is too small to accommodate everyone, so Manny and Francisco's two companions eat at the desk in the rectory. Mariano updates Francisco on the scandalous events involving Paul as the two talk at the end of the dining table.

After being fully briefed, Francisco asks to meet with Rita's father, who is the head of his family and the decision-maker. He is trying to head off an international scandal that originated in Rome, especially after Alphonso's unfortunate death. More importantly, he wants to know where Paul is and how Paul, God's chosen for the gift of stigmata and bilocation, could do such a thing. He feels there must be a tangible reason that will explain it all.

27

JOHNNY MEETS
THE SUPERIOR GENERAL'S "CREW"

Paul and Rita have run off to Rhode Island. Rita picked the resort town of Narragansett, a small, picturesque beachfront town with shops and restaurants. Its population swells with tourists during the summer months. She had considered going there with her husband, but her heart was not in it. However, her heart, mind, and body are all into being there with Paul. They've lost themselves in the town for the last three days in love's pure bliss. Rita treasures every second with Paul after being away from him for so many years.

The weather is being cooperative—sunny, high seventies. They hold hands, and she hugs him every chance she gets. She tells him of her loneliness without him and the empty feelings she felt for her husband. Paul is very attentive to her, reciprocating her feelings and talking of his lonely nights without her.

Their love is euphoric and at its highest peak, but soon it will be disrupted. Little do they realize Rita's father has called her credit card company and asked for her most recent transactions. He was refused, but his connections with the police in the 48th Precinct in the Bronx will soon produce the results he seeks.

Francisco has the monsignor call Rita's father and tell him he would like him to meet with a high-ranking official from the Vatican, who was sent there to resolve the incident involving his daughter.

Rita's father leaves his pastry shop and walks two blocks down to the church, where he is led into the same office where his daughter and Paul met for "counseling."

"*Buon giorno*, Signore Signorelli," Francisco says, wishing Rita's father "good morning" in Italian as he tries to get a feel for the man.

Vito acknowledges Francisco's words with a nod, an eager look on his face that indicates he wants to get down to business.

"I am here on behalf of the Vatican in Rome," Francisco says. "I was sent to resolve this matter with your daughter. I would like to begin by expressing our deepest sorrow."

Vito nods quickly in acknowledgment. "So, when do I get my daughter back?" he says in an Italian accent. He slaps the desk in anger. "Tell me when!"

Manny and the other two priests from the Vatican enter the small office and stare at Vito. Thinking they are ordinary priests, he starts to become more menacing in his actions. Then one of Francisco's priests grabs the nape of his neck and drives him back into his seat, keeping his forceful grip on Vito's shoulder.

Vito looks around in confusion. "What is this?"

"I ask that you give me a chance to resolve this problem," Francisco says, his voice calm. "I need forty-eight hours to do so."

Puzzled, but wanting to get his daughter back, Vito nods. "Okay. I give you the forty-eight hours, but after that, I take things into my own hands."

He gets up and walks out, as if he is in charge.

Francisco turns to Mariano. "Is there any place that Paul visited while he was here?"

The monsignor thinks for a moment before answering and then nods. "Yes, Mrs. Ciminetti's house, something to do with prayers being answered. I don't know much about it. He never talked to me about the things he was pursuing."

Francisco lets out a long slow sigh. "Then we must go to Mrs. Ciminetti's house."

All of them Jesuits, they are dressed traditionally in long black cassock robes with thirty-three buttons, a tribute to the life of Christ, except for the monsignor, who is a Franciscan priest. Francisco, the monsignor, Manny, and the other two priests stride down 187th Street and through the streets of the Bronx's Belmont section. They reach the corner of Cambrelling Avenue and make a left turn just before they reach 189th Street and stop at the Ciminetti house.

Bulldog and Murphy are amazed by the number of priests. "What's with all the Jesuits?" Murphy asks as their eyes stay glued to Philomena's front door.

As the monsignor rings the bell, he can't help but think the poor woman has already been through enough. A moment later, the door opens.

"Monsignor," Philomena says. "What's the matter? Why so many priests?" she asks, craning her neck to see them all.

"I'm sorry, Mrs. Ciminetti. This is the Superior General from Rome. He would like to speak to you."

"Yes, come in," she says, moving aside so they can enter.

As soon as they step inside, all the crucifixes in her house turn upside down, and the glass candle holders from her shrine smash against the floor.

The priests all stop and look at each other. They know exactly what is responsible.

Francisco turns to Manny and nods. "We are on the right trail."

Monsignor Mariano is frozen in place. He has never seen such a raw display of evil.

"I don't know what just happened," Philomena says. "I'm sorry. My great-granddaughter must have been playing by the candles. Please, come in and sit down."

She leads everyone into her small parlor and then goes around to all the crucifixes and straightens them.

"What can I help you with?" she asks as she makes a pot of espresso.

"Have you heard from my young colleague, Paul?" Francisco asks.

"Why, no," she says, appearing puzzled. "Is he all right?"

Francisco shakes his head. "We seem to have lost touch with him."

Just then, Johnny comes down the stairs and enters the room. "What's all this?" He looks at the Superior General and the others, all dressed in black. "Are you guys going to pull a heist or what?"

Francisco is not in the mood for Johnny's remarks or wasting time. "This is official church business. Stay out of it."

Johnny's temper flares. "Don't you ever talk to me like that, especially in my house." He approaches Francisco, his hand reaching behind his back.

Manny and one of the other two priests pull out daggers and step between Johnny and the Superior General. The other priest positions himself behind Johnny, who is reaching for a gun in the small of his back. Philomena screams in terror.

"Manny, no!" Francisco yells.

All movement stops. Johnny looks around with hard eyes. "Priests with knives? What the fuck is this?" He hasn't seen this kind of militant protection since the old Mafia bosses reigned. He nods at Francisco. "Who are you?"

Taking a deep breath, Francisco lets out a sigh of annoyance at having to talk to Johnny. "I am the Superior General of the Jesuit Order. I answer only to the Pope, and I will—we will . . ." He flashes his eyes at the three others, who put their daggers away. "We will do anything necessary to protect the Pope and the Catholic Church."

Johnny feels instant respect for the group of priests, who believe in something so much they are willing to die for it—and kill for it. "Why are you here?"

"I'm looking for one of my men, Paul," Francisco replies.

"You mean Allie Boy's kid brother?"

The Superior General gives Johnny a blank stare. "I don't know him as that. I know him only as Paul."

Johnny nods. "I heard that Paul came back for the love of his life, and he ran off with her . . . Vito's daughter."

"I am unconvinced of that," Francisco replies. "Do you know where Paul is?"

"No, but I can look into it."

Francisco sees the jailhouse street thug in Johnny. Yes, he has that right but not his degree of moral fiber.

"Hmm . . . I have had to deal with people with backgrounds like yours all over the world. What do you require for helping us, money?"

Johnny frowns, insulted at the insinuation. "I'm not who you think I am. I want nothing from you. If I can help you, I will."

Francisco senses Johnny's moral compass and rugged pride. "Okay then, can you 'look into it,' as you say? It will be greatly appreciated by the Church."

Johnny nods, feeling an instant kinship with the ballsy priests and the Superior General. The old man has a crew. They are down to earth. They are willing to kill and even die for the Superior General. Impressive.

28

JOHNNY PUTS OFF TOMAS—AGAIN

Johnny heads out and walks through the streets of his old neighborhood, not caring if the detectives outside see him or follow him. He arrives at Tommaso's restaurant. Tomas gives him a big hello and a hug and kiss on the cheek. He invites Johnny to a table and tells his waiter to bring food and drinks.

"So, have you finally decided to join us?" Tomas asks.

"I'm still getting used to being home and getting settled in," Johnny says. "I need a little more time to get situated."

Tommaso smiles. "Okay, let me know. The family has big things planned for you."

As the food and drink arrive, Johnny turns to the old man. "Tomas, do you know where the pastry guy's daughter is with the priest?"

Tomas smiles. "Why do you want to know that?" He picks up a small chunk of hard, sharp, dry Parmigiano-Reggiano cheese and places it in his mouth, followed by a sip of red wine. "You were never into neighborhood gossip."

Johnny chuckles. "The information can be helpful to friends of my mother, who are looking for Paul, the priest. Allie's kid brother."

Tomas looks at Johnny with one eye closed, then turns his head to the side, pausing to think. Then he turns back to Johnny and nods. "If it's important to you, I can find out."

Johnny smiles. "It would be very helpful."

Tomas summons one of the men at the bar and whispers into his ear. Soon, a lieutenant from the 48th Precinct arrives and slips a note to the man at the bar. Once the lieutenant leaves, the note is passed to Tomas, who slides it across the table to Johnny. Johnny is amazed by the speed of Tommaso's contacts.

"You know now if I call for you, you have to come," the old man says, his fingers still on the slip of paper.

Johnny knows exactly what he means. He is obligated to repay the favor. Johnny smiles slightly as he nods. "I never questioned that for a second."

Tommaso lifts his hand and lets Johnny have the note.

After finishing his dessert, Johnny bids Tommaso goodbye and thanks him for his help.

On the way back to his house, Bulldog and Patrick Murphy follow Johnny, but he ignores them.

"Were you successful in your little mission for the Church?" Francisco asks anxiously as soon as Johnny is inside.

"I was," Johnny says, nodding. He passes the slip of paper to the Superior General. The information was meant for Vito, Rita's father, who would have already been on his way, along with his two sons, but Tommaso and Johnny have intercepted it.

29

CAUGHT ON CAMERA?

A short time later, having borrowed the monsignor's car, Francisco and the three priests race up the New York State Thruway and travel on Interstate 95 into Connecticut and into Narragansett, Rhode Island.

When they arrive at the inn, they go to the front desk and ask for the manager. He is a short, stocky man with a comb-over, dyed black hair, and a thick black mustache.

"Can I help you?"

"Are you a Catholic?" Francisco asks.

The manager frowns. "What do my religious beliefs have to do with anything?"

"There was a priest here," Francisco replies, "with a woman."

"When did he check in?"

"Two nights ago. The woman's name is Rita Giovanelli, but she could be going by her maiden name, Signorelli."

The manager thinks for a moment. "Oh, yes, I recall that pair. They came early in the morning and were very much in love." He pauses, realizing the implications. "He is a priest?"

Francisco ignores the manager's question. "Are they still here?"

"No, they checked out this morning."

"Do you have any video footage of them?" Manny asks.

"I'm sure we do. Give me a minute to look."

The men sit around in the inn's lobby, looking at magazines and watching the shoreline as the waves crash against the beach and then roll lazily back into the ocean. The beautiful beach property behind the inn is magnetic.

A few minutes later, the manager returns with a disc, places it into a video player, and points to the screen above the front desk. It clearly shows an image of Paul and Rita talking and then Paul leaning in and giving Rita a peck on her lips as he holds her hands and stares intensely into her eyes.

A moment later, Francisco shakes his head. "That's not Paul."

Manny looks at him in disbelief. "Forgive me, Superior General, but that most certainly is Paul."

Francisco shakes his head vigorously. "No, Manny, it is not. Now, let's go back to New York."

Manny frowns in confusion, certain it is Paul in the video, as are the other two priests, but he is not about to defy his master. Instead, he bows his head in obedience. "Yes, Superior General."

30

RASHID HATCHES A PLAN

Rashid is puzzled by the fact that Reggie's father is still alive, how he has stopped Rashid from selling drugs, and how he has lost two of his best hit men. His girls are no longer able to turn tricks for him either. His money is quickly drying up.

In frustration, he beats Reggie until she is bloody and crying hysterically. Lena tries to stop him, but it's hopeless. Rashid punches, slaps, and kicks Reggie's ribs and face.

"Now, bitch, you're going to call your father and tell him you're in trouble, and that I'm going to hurt you very badly. And don't forget to tell him, 'Please, Daddy, I need you, please come help me'!"

He dials the phone as she tries to stop crying from the pain and the swelling of her face and eyes. The blood pouring from her nose and from over her eye gushes all over her hair and face.

"Hello," Johnny says.

Reggie winces as she tells him the message. Despite her hysteria, she manages to blurt, "*E' una trappola* (It's a trap)," right before Rashid hangs up. He doesn't catch her warning to her father, and he goes off to prepare for Johnny to walk into his trap.

After hanging up, Johnny goes down to his basement, yanks open the drawer in the basement wall, and pulls out his killing tools. He also puts on a long coat that has oversized pockets sewed inside of it to fit his tools of death. Inside the pockets, he places a sawed-off shotgun, two pistols—one automatic and one revolver—and two grenades.

He climbs onto the roof of his house, then climbs down the side and disappears into the darkness of the neighborhood alleyways.

Before long, he is on the roof directly across the street from Rashid's building on Crotona Avenue. Looking down into the courtyard, Johnny sees Rashid has two pit bulls outside in the back alley and two more on the roof of his building. The ones on the roof are unchained. If Johnny comes up through the alley or across onto the roof, the dogs will attack, causing a great deal of ruckus, giving away his position.

Two of Rashid's toughest, most street-smart men stand guard in the courtyard, ready for battle. They are armed with .380 caliber automatic pistols.

After doing reconnaissance, Johnny returns home and grabs some of the cut-up pieces of Rashid's assassins from his freezer. He takes ten pounds of meat and sprinkles it with a crushed-up bottle of sleeping pills. Then he returns to the back alley, where the two pit bulls are. Rashid keeps them hungry so they stay mean and alert.

As Johnny approaches, the dogs let out a low growl and bare their teeth. He throws a piece of meat to each of them, which they gobble up. He throws more meat, about half the bag, and they devour it. Then he waits for the sleeping pills to take effect.

Minutes later, the first pit bull stumbles and then lies down on its side, unconscious. The other dog also becomes lethargic and then collapses into a deep sleep.

In a flash, Johnny flies up the fire escape. On the roof, he repeats the process until those dogs pass out, too. Then he climbs down the fire escape leading to the apartment where Reggie is being kept.

Staying to the side of her window, he peeks into another window, so quickly that no one inside would notice. Satisfied the room is clear, he pulls out a small crowbar and pops the lock. He is about to open the window and enter when he hears Rashid's voice. He ducks to the side of the window again.

Rashid enters the room and looks around, glancing down at the courtyard before returning to his ambush position. Johnny, who is watching him with the help of a dentist's mirror attached to a long, thin metal handle, can tell Rashid is on edge.

Johnny opens the window and slips inside the apartment. He finds Reggie asleep. Lena is awake though, still holding Reggie in her arms. She recognizes Johnny from pictures Reggie has shown her, so she is not alarmed. He puts his finger on his lips, and she nods.

Johnny relaxes his grip on his gun. He was ready to pull the trigger of the silenced weapon if she was uncooperative and tried to alert Rashid.

Rashid calls Lena to get him a beer out of the refrigerator. Johnny motions for her to stay put. Then he walks over to the fridge, opens it, pauses for a second, and then closes it, pretending to get Rashid a beer. He peeks out from the kitchen, sees Rashid looking intensely into the courtyard, and then approaches him. He walks lightly to simulate the sounds of a woman. When he gets close enough, he aims his pistol at Rashid's head.

"I wish we had more time so I could do this right," Johnny says.

Rashid moves to react, but Johnny squeezes the trigger, which is pointed right behind Rashid's ear, so the bullet will do maximum damage, an old Mafia-style trick. Rashid drops to the floor like a heap of junk. It is all over in the blink of an eye.

Johnny walks back to the bedroom, awakens Reggie, and hugs her. "Daddy's here, baby. Time to come home."

She hugs him back, crying. Lena stands there, not knowing what will happen to her.

"Daddy, take her," Reggie says.

He looks at two girls and sees a bond of friendship has been established. He nods. "Okay, move fast."

He takes them up to the roof, but Reggie is unable to climb down the fire escape due to the severe beating she just received. Johnny thinks quickly. Time is running out. The dogs will be awake soon.

He walks to the edge of the roof and looks down at the two bodyguards. They are directly under Rashid's third-floor window. He runs back into the apartment, leaving Lena and Reggie on the roof.

Once there, he lifts Rashid's body and throws it out the window. It lands at the bodyguards' feet with a thunderous thump. His head cracks open, and brain matter and thick blood splatter out.

"Oh, shit! I am out this motherfucker!" the tall, thin bodyguard says, looking up at the shattered window. He drops his gun and runs out of the courtyard and down the street.

"Rashid!" the other screams. "Who did this shit to you? I'm going to kill that motherfucker." He pulls out his gun and runs into the building.

When he reaches Rashid's apartment, the young thug kicks open the door, catching Johnny off-guard and knocking the gun from his hand. The thug attacks him. He is strong and many years younger than Johnny, who has a tough time in the battle.

The thug gets on top of Johnny and tries to point his gun at the back of Johnny's head, but Johnny keeps moving his head from side to side. He knows what the younger man is trying to do. He tries to grip his genitals, but the struggle is too fierce.

Johnny finally breaks free and grabs the thug's gun hand. He kicks at the thug, and the thug kicks back. He is a tough individual determined to get revenge for Rashid's death.

The thug pushes Johnny backward, and he hits the window through which Johnny threw Rashid's body. The remaining windowpane shatters, and shards of glass land on Rashid's body below.

Johnny begins to weaken and tire. His age cannot be denied. As he hangs out the window, he reaches into his pocket, pulls out a grenade, and puts it to his teeth. The pin drops out, and he places it in the window sill.

The thug aims his gun at Johnny's head. "You're a—"

Johnny lets go of the windowsill and plummets to the ground. A second later, the grenade detonates. As Johnny lands on Rashid's body, a fireball erupts inside the apartment, tearing the man's torso in half. The top part of his body lies across the windowsill, his hand still clutching his gun.

Rashid's body broke Johnny's fall, but he is still badly injured. He staggers to his feet and sees Lena leading Reggie down the final few steps of the stairs into the courtyard between the two buildings. Lena had decided to take the stairs, helping Reggie all the way down. He leads them back into an alley and takes his beloved Reginella home as police sirens wail in the distance.

Entering through the cellar door, Lena and Reggie help Johnny up the stairs to his bedroom and into bed.

Hearing Reggie's voice, Philomena comes out of her room. As soon as she sees her granddaughter, they embrace, tears of joy running down all three women's faces. The uproar wakes up young Philomena, and she joins in the happy reunion.

Content in his quest for revenge, and thankful to have his daughter back home, Johnny lies in bed, pretending not to notice any of it. He is a hardcore, old-school gangster, but the joyous scene warms even his callous heart.

31

PRAYERS ANSWERED

The next morning, Philomena is up bright and early, waiting for the local florist shop to open on Crescent Avenue. The owner's name is Jimmy "Peppers" Cersoula, a short, stocky, old Italian man who always has the butt of an old Italian De Nobili cigar in his mouth.

As soon as he opens his store, Philomena approaches him. "Jimmy, I'd like one dozen of your best red roses."

Still feeling the effects of drinking too much homemade Italian wine the night before, Jimmy is grumpy. "You want to wait a minute? I haven't even put the key in the door yet."

"Hurry, Jimmy! Mother Mary is waiting for these."

Realizing her intent, he tips his hat to Philomena in a sign of respect for the Blessed Mother. "Coming right up, Philomena! One dozen of my best right away!"

Roses in hand, she walks briskly to Mount Carmel and places the flowers in front of the statue of Mary. After kissing the statue's feet, she kneels with her rosary beads in hand. "Thank you for answering my prayer. I am so happy in my life." She makes the sign of the cross and then stands up.

As she goes to leave, a single drop of clear water hits her hand, and the scent of fresh flowers fills her senses. She looks at the statue's face and sees the moisture traveling the same way the previous tears flowed. It is an acknowledgment of her miracle. Philomena knows it to be so.

32

THE FACE OF THE ENEMY

Francisco is having trouble sleeping after losing Paul. It is disturbing and upsetting. He keeps wondering where he went wrong and if he's missing something.

He hears a muffled cry. It sounds like it's coming from outside. He listens and hears the cry again.

"Paul?" he whispers. He gets up and follows the sound. It leads him up a narrow set of wooden stairs to the loft in the back of the church, where the organ plays and the choir sings. He sees a man in a hooded shirt with his back facing him.

"Paul?"

The man begins to walk away. Francisco follows. "Paul, stop!"

Suddenly, the man halts, and Francisco approaches him. "Paul, where have you been?"

The man neither responds nor turns around.

"Where have you been, Paul?"

Finally, the man turns and looks directly at Francisco. Then he smashes his hand against Francisco's face, knocking him to the ground and sending his glasses skittering across the floor.

The man's face is stony, his skin a grayish color. His piercing eyes are black and deep in his face. His nose is long and narrow with wide, flaring nostrils, and his frame is lanky and long.

"I am not your Paul!" The strange man points his finger at Francisco. "Hear me, old man. I give you warning. Leave here. Do not go beyond the point from where you are."

Francisco struggles to his feet, leaning on the organ. "Who are you?"

"I reign here on Earth. It is my soul you seek to take."

"I am here to do God's work, and I am only obeying his will," Francisco protests.

"He reigns in heaven!" the man screams. "I reign here on Earth, for it is I who will take the world's souls. You will take orders from me while here on Earth."

"I will never take orders from you!" Francisco says.

The organ pipes begin to clang loudly, and the organ starts to shake. It plays louder and louder until it falls from its perch, knocking Francisco to the floor. The figure points his finger at the Superior General. He opens his mouth, and the voices of people Francisco knows to be dead come out. "Francisco, this is your last warning. This is not any of your business. Leave here, or face the fires of his wrath."

The voices send a chill through Francisco's nervous system, paralyzing his thoughts.

Looking into the face of the strange and frightening man, he sees a deep never-ending forest of so many souls of priests and cardinals that he knew throughout the years, screaming and burning in the fires in hell, calling his name and asking for his help. He also sees all the sins he has committed throughout his life. Finally, he looks away, unable to bear it any longer.

He becomes intensely ill, gripped with fear for his soul. The winds of dread blow over him, bringing him to his knees. He feels the hands and hears the voices of the clergy and sees their faces pulling him down. Lying on the floor, he crawls over them, fighting their grip as he reaches toward a large crucifix hanging from the ceiling in the front of the altar.

"Oh, Mary, please help me! Please forgive me, dear Lord, if I have sinned! Oh, dearest and most merciful Lord, please help me and take me into your kingdom now at this very second!" His fear of going to hell with Lucifer is all-consuming.

Francisco hears footsteps climbing the steps that lead into the organ chamber. The footsteps stop, and the shadow of a person appears. The man extends his arm, twists his hand, palm down, and a single drop of blood falls to the floor. The moment it makes contact, a powerful blast of unbridled energy blows through the chamber and beyond, leaving a feeling of peace and calm in its wake. Then the stranger, Paul, stands ready to do battle with the devil.

"You leave here!" the hooded man screams.

Paul calmly dips his finger into his open wound and, with a shake of his wrist, sprinkles blood on the hooded man, who screams in pain in a thousand different voices.

"Your pain is caused by him who has cast you out!" Paul shouts in a loud, defiant, and authoritative tone. "The pain of the blood of the purest and holiest is why you cry out. It is he who is superior and righteous and without fear that causes you pain. Be gone from here, Satan!"

Paul points at Francisco. "His soul belongs to his Savior, our Lord. You cannot bear false claim to it, for it is true that Michael, the Archangel, will come down and, in all of his magnificence, he will crush you and send you back into the bowels of hell. It is all foretold by the Creator. This is where you will remain for the rest of eternity."

The evil one screams in pain. "Fuck you! Your savior will not save even one soul I claim, your soul included. You will join me in hell."

In response, Paul douses him with another blast of the blood from his wounds. "Do not pretend you are greater than him! He reigns supreme, for it is he, the Father and the Creator of all, in heaven and on Earth. He even created you, and when you rose against him, he cast you out of heaven to reign in the world of darkness. Once again, you commit the same sin against him. Hear me, evil one: The battle is coming, and you cannot stop it. You will lose so many souls to heaven, for the Messenger is coming. He will announce the Second Coming of the anointed one. He will warn the people of the world to repent, for the Second Coming is at hand."

The evil figure stands straight up and grows in stature, transforming into someone of astonishing beauty. He is Lucifer, the angel God created, the angel who betrayed God and tried to take over his kingdom. Satan becomes so beautiful that Francisco cannot bear to look upon him any longer, feeling so ugly in comparison.

"Paul," Satan says in a soothing, seductive voice, "come with me. Help me destroy the Messenger. I will create a lifetime of beauty and wonders for you in my kingdom."

Though amazed by Satan's beauty, Paul blasts him again with another splatter of blood from his wounds. "May the beauty of the Lord our God be upon me. The Lord, in all his beauty and majesty, will always be with me and I with him. It is the Father who cast you out. It is Jesus who said to you, 'Get behind me, Satan.' Now it is I who say to you, leave this place, for it is he who allows me the power to command you to do this."

"Paul, you have taken your last breath on Earth!" Satan cries. "I am going to extinguish you, and your soul will be with me."

"No!" Paul replies. "I will be with the one who has served his Father well on Earth and with whom the Father is pleased. It is promised to all those who seek the Lord's forgiveness. We all will dwell in the house of the Lord for eternity. It is you, Satan, who will never again be in heaven, for you have caused the wickedest of sins. You will spend eternity in the most wretched of places—your hell—so, be gone to it."

The menacing figure dissipates and crumbles, leaving behind a cloud of smoke and the agonizing smell of sulfur.

Paul helps Francisco to his feet.

"Am I going to be in hell?" Francisco asks, his voice shaking.

"No!" Paul replies. "You will not. You have served the Lord our God. You have fought the fires of Satan with fire in the service of the Lord. Take joy in knowing the Lord has a place for you in his kingdom."

Francisco feels much-needed relief, his intense fear retreating. One more second, and he would have had a stroke or a massive heart attack. He hangs his head, makes the sign of the cross, and then looks up. "Thank you, Lord." Drained of strength, he allows Paul to help him back to his quarters.

Paul applies a cold compress to Francisco's face, tending to his wounds, as he lies in his bed.

"Where did you go?" Francisco asks, his voice weak.

"I was with the holiest of the holy. He has called to me. I was on the most amazing trip through his gift of bilocation. He has clarified the mission. It is to protect the Messenger from Satan, who is trying to destroy him."

"When is the Messenger going to come?"

"He is already here."

Francisco begins to weep, knowing the Messenger has arrived to tell of Jesus's return to the world. The Second Coming will soon be at hand. The end is near, Armageddon. He knows that Satan has shown himself, because he does not want the Messenger to fulfill the Scriptures. If there is no Messenger, Satan cannot be defeated by Michael, the Archangel, who will cast him into hell for eternity. If Satan can eliminate the Messenger, it will delay Jesus' Second Coming, because the prophecy will not be fulfilled.

The Messenger's warning will be of the return of the anointed one, telling all who will listen to repent and be saved.

Paul repeats his answer with a blank stare. "He is already here." Then he rests his hand on the Superior General's shoulder to console him.

33

NEW LIFE

Driving back from Narragansett, Rita's love bliss continues. She holds Paul's hand as he drives. She reminisces about what they would have done and how they would have started a home and a family. She smiles at him. "I want to be pregnant by you."

He touches her stomach. "You already are."

She laughs. "I wish."

"You can stop wishing," he says. "You really are."

She makes a funny face and brushes it off as a bad joke.

Farther down the road, the news comes on the radio that Iran has signed a deal with the United States that allows them to have nuclear power for peaceful means. Just then, a violent eruption happens inside Rita's belly.

She turns to Paul, her eyes wide. "I just felt a fierce movement inside of me, like a baby kicking!"

Paul smiles. "Elijah is itching to get out and preach to the world."

Rita looks at Paul. "You know, you're starting to scare me. Would you stop that, please?"

"Okay."

"Thank you!"

As she looks out the window, another news report comes on saying that Iran has made a deal with the approval of the president of the United States. Again, she feels a wild and explosive movement inside her womb.

"I think I need to see a doctor about this," she says, holding her stomach. "You're really beginning to freak me out. I don't want to hear about this anymore—about Elijah or any of that Second Coming stuff. This movement in my stomach is starting to worry me."

"Okay, let's get you to a doctor," Paul says.

On the way home, they stop at an urgent-care center in Stanford, Connecticut. As they sit in the waiting room, she leans her head on Paul's shoulder, and he holds her hand.

A door leading into the back office opens, and a girl wearing blue scrubs calls Rita's name and then leads them into the doctor's office, placing Rita's folder in a rack outside the door.

A moment later, a young doctor walks in. "Hello. I'm Dr. Dominick Carello. You're getting pains in your stomach? Can you lie down on the table?"

She does, and he begins to press in the area that she complains about. He feels kicking. She jumps.

He pauses his examination and looks at her. "Have you been trying to get pregnant?"

Rita laughs. "No, not yet."

"Well, I'll send you for a sonogram anyway."

Rita gives Paul a troubled look.

A few minutes later, in the next office, a young female technician rubs clear gel on Rita's stomach and then begins the exam. "Do you want a picture of him?"

Rita looks at her, stunned. "What picture? Of who?"

The technician smiles. "Congratulations! You're having a son."

Rita's mouth opens in shock. "A son? I can't be pregnant!" She glances at Paul. The technician looks puzzled by Rita's reaction to the good news. "Oh no, you're about three months along."

Rita shakes her head in disbelief. "I don't understand it. There must be some mistake." She glances at Paul with an astounded look on her face. "Was I asleep? We didn't . . ." She points at her stomach, making a circular motion. Paul looks at her and shakes his head.

"No, there's no mistake," the technician says. She smiles. "Maybe it's divine intervention."

"Yes, it was," Paul says.

The technician gives him an awkward look. She was only joking, but Paul sounds serious. She starts putting her tools away. "In any case, you better get ready. You're going to have a baby."

34

ARE TWO PAULS BETTER THAN ONE?

In the parking lot outside the doctor's office, Paul holds Rita's hand as she weeps. "We've been chosen by God to do his work on Earth," he says, trying to comfort her. "You are now a part of something that is greater than anything else. It's an honor, and you will be rewarded in heaven."

Rita looks at him, her eyes red from crying. "My father is going to kill me. Kill me, understand? Can we say it's my husband's? We'll say that just before he died, I became pregnant. Then my dad will accept it."

Paul shakes his head. "No. He died too long ago for that. Besides, somehow, I don't think the Lord would be pleased."

He looks into her eyes and tells her that the baby she is carrying is the Messenger, the chosen one sent to Earth to tell people to prepare for the Second Coming. All of this is in the Bible and must be fulfilled. "Satan knows the Messenger is here, and he will try to destroy him, so he can have the souls of all the unsuspecting people who don't know the Second Coming is near. He is here to save their souls before it's too late. It is God's last warning. We must heed it, or they will die with unclean souls and go into the fires of hell. We will be taking the souls from Satan. All those who repent will enter heaven, the Lord's kingdom."

Rita doesn't believe anything Paul is telling her, thinking there must be a logical explanation for why she is pregnant. "I'll wait to see my doctor when I get home," she says. "This may just be a tumor or something else. It can't be a baby."

Undaunted, Paul tells her the Messenger's name, Elijah. "You must come to Rome and live inside the Vatican until he is born. You will both be safe there. He is coming soon."

Rita stares at him in disbelief. "Are you nuts?"

Suddenly, she thinks maybe she would have been better off without Paul back in her life.

They arrive back in the Bronx, where she intends to drop off Paul. She is preparing herself mentally for the drive back to the suburbs to try to explain her absence, thinking she has made a terrible mistake by getting back together with Paul.

When she pulls up in front of Mount Carmel Church, Paul invites her in. She wants to leave, but something draws her inside.

They enter the church rectory. Mrs. Arceola stares at them in shock, as do the monsignor and the Superior General. Unfazed, Paul says hello to everyone. As they walk into the back of the rectory, Rita looks at Paul. "Why are we walking back here?"

"Because I want you to meet someone."

A man has his back to them as they enter the hallway that separates the offices in the rectory. He turns around and looks at her.

Rita's eyes go wide, and she turns to Paul. "How did you get in front of me?"

As she turns to look back, she sees Paul in front of her and behind her at the same time. She gasps. "Am I losing my mind?"

"No, you are seeing two of us," they say in unison. "It is a gift that God gave me when he chose me for his work."

"I have the gift of bilocation," the Paul in front of her says. "I'm able to be in two places at once."

He shows her his stigmata wounds. Then she turns to talk to the Paul behind her, but he dissipates into oblivion. She looks back at the new Paul. Then she becomes dizzy and passes out.

Paul catches her, and he and two nuns help her to a room and tend to her.

35

VITO'S ULTIMATUM

One of Vito's friends tells him he saw Rita enter the church with Paul. Vito and two of his sons run to Mount Carmel. He demands to see his daughter. Francisco asks Vito to come into the office, so he can explain.

"Where's my daughter?" Vito says. "I want to take her home right now."

Francisco tries to reason with the raging man in Italian. "You will, but you must understand that your daughter is pregnant. She was chosen by God to be part of a very important mission."

"No, stop all this bullshit by Paul. Give me my daughter, or I call the cops."

Francisco informs Vito that Rita is carrying a gift of God for the masses of the world. This is a very important baby to the Church and to humanity. "If you take her from here, then you will be responsible for the loss of possibly millions of souls."

"No! Fuck this bullshit. Give me my daughter, now!" Vito yells, red-faced with anger.

Francisco looks at Paul and Manny and the other two priests. "Okay," he says reluctantly. "Bring her here."

They bring Rita to the front of the rectory. Vito grabs her and draws his hand back to hit her in her face, but one of the priests quickly overpowers him. When one of Vito's sons tries to intervene, Manny grabs him in a chokehold. The other assassin priest locks Vito's other son in a similar chokehold, stopping him.

"Get your fuckin' hands off me and my family!" Vito yells.

Francisco nods for his priests to obey.

Vito walks over to Rita and points his finger at her. "Rita, *vieni a casa, vieni a casa con me*! (Come home with me right now!)"

129

She trembles as she follows him out of the rectory.

Francisco instructs Manny and one of his men to follow and make sure no harm comes to her.

Outside, Vito curses in Italian, gripped by an uncontrollable rage. Manny and the other priest step between Rita and her father. He continues to yell, but is unable to get within striking range.

Rita has had enough. She runs for her car and takes off to her home in Rockland County, some forty miles away.

Vito screams with rage and then stomps down the street, his sons behind him.

Once inside his bakery, Vito cools off and then orders his wife to call Rita and tell her he has calmed down. "I will go up to see her."

He jumps in his station wagon and takes his oldest son, Emilio, with him. He drives up the Sprain Brook Parkway and over the Mario Cuomo/Tappan Zee Bridge, heading into New City, New York, pulling up in front of Rita's house.

Inside, she is vomiting, in full pregnancy sickness mode, but she opens the front door and lets them in.

Vito grabs her arm and squeezes it, hurting her. "What the fuck did you do? Huh, *puttana*? You are a whore! You pregnant?"

She refuses to respond.

"You answer me, you fuckin' *puttana*! Are you?"

She looks back at him defiantly. "Yes!"

He slaps her face and pulls her hair. Emilio joins in. "You stupid fuck! Your reputation is ruined! What are all my friends going to say about our family?"

"You get rid of this baby!" Vito says. "You go to the abortion place tomorrow, first thing, and get rid of it. I'll take you tomorrow. You understand me?"

She nods, trembling in fear as tears run down her face.

The two men storm out.

36

A Desperate Plan

The next morning at 3 a.m., as soon as she feels the baby kicking again, Rita's motherly instincts kick in, and she feels the need to protect her unborn child. She calls Paul at the church and tells him of her father's intentions. Paul relays the information to Francisco.

Three hours later, Vito wakes up to do his baking. He goes to the corner Italian coffee shop across the street from his bakery, which opens at 6 a.m. to service all the tradesmen, construction workers, and laborers, some of whom have a shot or two of scotch in their espresso to start their day. Vito is one of them.

He sips his espresso and then turns away and sets his cup down when someone calls his name. As Vito engages in conversation, the assassin priest pretends to reach for something but instead drops a white powdery substance into Vito's cup, his actions hidden by the sleeve of his robe. Vito finishes his coffee and leaves, the assassin priest not far behind.

The priest waits and observes from across the street. Twenty minutes later, police and firemen arrive, along with an ambulance. Vito is carried out on a stretcher. The priest leaves and heads back to Mount Carmel Church, only two blocks away. Satan will have to find another way to destroy the Messenger.

He reports to the Superior General. With Rita's father in the hospital for symptoms related to a perforated ulcer or appendicitis, Francisco and Paul know they must act quickly to get Rita within the safety of the Vatican's walls. Rita can stay there until she gives birth without having to be processed through immigration, due to diplomatic immunity. The delay will be long enough for the Messenger to be born.

Paul, Manny, and the two assassin priests need to get back up to Ri-

131

ta's house. Francisco gets a parishioner from Mount Carmel Church to help. Joey Calavolpe, a religious man with a passion for God and the Church, owns a large white commuter van, which he uses for deliveries for his pastry shop. His insignia is on the side of the van, "Joseph Calavolpe Pastry Bronx, New York." He gladly takes them to Rita's house.

Paul tells Rita to pack her belongings and her passport and to be ready to leave. She is waiting outside with all her luggage when they pull up. Soon, they are on their way back to Mount Carmel to gather their things and then go off to JFK Airport for the flight to Rome.

Vito gets out of the hospital and calls the police to report that Rita has been kidnapped. Using his connection with the 48th Precinct, he gets some high-ranking NYPD police officials to come to Mount Carmel and interrogate the monsignor. He refuses to say anything to the police, claiming all that was told to him was in the way of confession, and he cannot reveal anything to them. It is canon law, and it is his duty as a priest not to reveal anything told to him in confession.

When they are three blocks away from Mount Carmel, on 187th Street, Joey sees the police cars in front of the church. "Something really bad must be happening," he says. "Look at all the police."

Francisco looks at Paul and nods, knowing it's for them. He tries to come up with a plan. Then he remembers Philomena's house is up the block. "Joseph, can you please make a right down this street?"

"Of course, Father," Joey says, turning onto Cambrelling Avenue.

Francisco asks him to stop in front of Philomena's house. He and Paul get out and ring the doorbell. Reggie answers, Philomena right behind her.

"Is your son home?" Francisco asks Philomena.

"Yes, but what's wrong?"

"I cannot say," Francisco replies. "We just need his help."

She goes up to Johnny's bedroom. He is still recovering from his fall. He lifts himself out of bed, wincing with pain, and limps to the door. "Yes, what's up?"

"The police are looking for us," Francisco says. "We need a place to stay."

"Okay, hurry up," Johnny says, his street instinct kicking in. "Go around the corner behind my house. I'll come and get you."

Johnny has heard all the sirens passing by his house on the way to Mount Carmel. He knows the two cops watching his house will see them come in and will sound the alarm when an all-points bulletin is put out for the fugitives.

The van empties out around the corner behind Johnny's house. Francisco pauses to thank Joey for his help.

"Father, can you give me a quick blessing?" Joey asks.

"Yes, Joe," Francisco says, anxious to get going, "but it will have to be quick." He gives a heartfelt blessing, looking into Joey's eyes and smiling warmly. "Thank you, Joe. You have been such a great help to the Church."

Joey smiles back. "Are you kidding, Father? Anytime. Here, take my number. Call me if you need anything. I am at your service twenty-four seven. We never sleep." He hands Francisco his business card. Then he pulls away from the curb.

As Francisco and the others enter Johnny's home, little Philomena is playing with her mother, Lena, Johnny, and her great-grandmother.

Philomena's life is now complete and happy, her bond with her God unbreakable. She has such a wonderful outlook on life with her entire family together. She begins cooking, adding more tomatoes to the sauce and bringing out more pasta, making enough meat sauce to feed everyone.

"What's going on?" Johnny asks as they all share pasta and wine.

Francisco wipes his mouth. "We are on a very important mission here, and the police are going to arrest us for kidnapping."

Johnny looks at Rita and Paul and then shakes his head. "I thought a priest couldn't be with a woman. What's she doing with him?"

Irritated at having to explain himself, Francisco looks up to the heavens. *Lord, I know I'm here to do your will, but must there be a lunatic involved?* He turns back to Johnny. "She's not with him. She is with God. We cannot use public airports; the police are going to stop us from leaving. We must get to Rome. Can you help us?"

Johnny tilts his head and tightens his lips. "I'm not sure, but I'll find out."

37

JOHNNY DEEPENS HIS OBLIGATION

Johnny goes to Tommaso's restaurant once again to ask him a favor. The old man laughs. "This is your second request this week. You are staying busy, huh?"

Embarrassed, Johnny smiles. "I wouldn't ask, but it's important."

Tommaso feels this could be a serious favor that could cause him trouble with the authorities. He motions with his eyes toward the back door. "Let's do a walk and talk." It's an extra precaution to avoid being recorded by authorities.

They walk along Arthur Avenue, a busy Italian-American street filled with Italian restaurants, butcher shops, pastry shops, bakeries, fishmongers, and cheese stores. It is bustling with people. Tommaso knows it will be impossible to pick up their conversation on a wiretap. He looks at Johnny. "What do you need?"

"I need to get six people to Rome. They're hot, and they can't leave the normal way. No public airports. They will be detained and arrested. They think it's kidnapping, and the FBI will be involved."

Tommaso looks at Johnny. "Do you know these people you're getting involved with? Do you have them with you?"

"There is no kidnapping here. And yes, they're with me," Johnny says.

Tommaso shakes his head as he searches for answers in his mind. Finally, he looks at Johnny. "I hope this means a lot to you, because this is a big favor, and it is going to cost." He rubs his index finger and his thumb together, meaning it will cost money. Then he smiles at his heir apparent. "I know you don't have it, so I will take care of it. Just have them ready. You'll need to get them to Teterboro Airport tonight at ten. You will meet with Big Sonny on Belmont Avenue, one block behind your house. You will have to get them there without being seen. You will need to find transportation for them and Big Sonny. He'll show you the way and what to do. I can get them as far as Canada. We still have a lot of friends up there. Then they will pretty much be home free. And Johnny, I hope this is important for you."

"It is, Tomas," Johnny says.

Tommaso smiles. "Did you hear? Large Louis and his son are no longer a part of this world? They were found dead in their hotel room in New Jersey. They must have pissed someone off. Large Louis and his son were going to be cooperating witnesses with the FBI, so they had to go. *Buona fortuna!*"

Johnny knows there is no way he can ever repay the old man for those murders and now this. He is deeply indebted to Tomas and will have to join his gang when this is all over.

Tommaso nods at Johnny. "Good piece of work. I mean, reuniting your daughter with your family."

Johnny smiles in response.

38

RACE FOR THE BORDER

Big Sonny, a.k.a. the Duke, waits on the corner of 189th Street and Belmont Avenue. Francisco has arranged with Joey to give them another lift. Night has fallen, and the cold wind makes it feel like fall, even though autumn is still months away.

Joey pulls up and nods to Big Sonny. The Duke is a tall well-built man with a full head of black hair. His black eyes are surrounded by gold wire-rimmed aviation-style glasses. His long, narrow nose and chiseled face make him a menacing figure. Joey is smaller in stature, has thinning hair, and a slightly wide nose from his days as a boxer and street brawler. He also wears accountant-type wire-rimmed glasses.

Big Sonny knows Joey from way back. When Joey was younger, he was a wild man with a quick temper who would get into fights for the smallest reason. But God came calling, and Joey has never wavered from his love for God and the Lord Jesus Christ. It is safe to say that his love and fire for God grows each day. Both men are united in their mission to get the Superior General and his three men, Paul, and Rita on a plane to Canada.

Johnny waves to Big Sonny, who opens the side door to Joey's van and waves the passengers to come. The men fill the back two rows of seats as Rita, Paul, and Francisco sit in the second row. Big Sonny and Joey sit up front.

"Where to, Father?" Joey asks.

"We're going to Jersey," Big Sonny says. "Head for the George Washington Bridge."

They head for the Bronx River Parkway South. Turning onto Fordham Road from Hughes Avenue, they pass Fordham University and then the Botanical Gardens and the Bronx Zoo on their way toward the George Washington Bridge.

Big Sonny notices a heavy police presence along the Cross Bronx Expressway heading toward the mouth of the bridge. He looks at Joey. "We can't go this way."

"Traffic isn't that bad," Joey says. "Do your best, and the Lord will do the rest."

Big Sonny realizes Joey is not up to speed on what is going on with his passengers, but he knows Joey is familiar with the ways of the streets. "They're hot," he says, jabbing his thumb toward the back of the van.

Joey looks in the rear-view mirror at all his passengers and then back at Big Sonny, who was a former cab driver and is now a loyal friend to Tommaso.

"Take it from me," Sonny says, looking at him over the top of his aviator sunglasses. "They're hot. We can't go through the checkpoint, or we'll get pinched."

Joey turns off at the Jerome Avenue exit and pulls under the elevated train tracks. Still a bit shocked, he waits as a train passes by overhead. After grasping the seriousness of the situation, he looks at Big Sonny. "Where do we go from here?"

Big Sonny looks at Joey with a solemn face, still peering over his aviator glasses. "Canada."

Joey looks at him and then turns and stares straight ahead, dumbfounded. He wasn't expecting this, but he can't leave the priests stranded. Being a deeply religious and devout Catholic, he makes the sign of the cross and asks the Superior General to ask the Lord for a safe passage. "Will you also please pray for my wife's understanding for me not being home tonight and for missing dinner?"

Everyone but Big Sonny makes the sign of the cross.

"Are you a non-believer?" Francisco asks.

Big Sonny looks back at him. "I'm Jewish."

Francisco nods and then raises his hands and closes his eyes. "Lord, please allow us to defeat the evils of darkness and grant us safe passage into Canada. May you give a special blessing to our Jewish friend, and may you grant . . ." He opens his eyes and looks at Joey. "Excuse me, Joe, but what is your wife's name?"

"My lovely wife of fifty years is Linda."

Francisco nods and then closes his eyes again. "And Lord, kindly protect Joey from Linda's rightful wrath of fury for him not being home tonight. We ask this through Christ, our Lord. Amen." He opens his eyes and winks at Joey.

Once again, everyone but Big Sonny makes the sign of the cross, but he looks back at Francisco and nods. "Thank you."

Francisco responds with a smile.

Joey heads north toward the Major Deegan Expressway. The priests are in tourist mode as they drive past Yankee Stadium toward the entrance to the Major Deegan Expressway, also known as Interstate 87, the road that will lead them straight to Canada, some seven hours away.

39

TROUBLING NEWS

Rita, her head resting on Paul's shoulder, falls asleep. The ordeal has been exhausting for her.

Joey is listening to a news radio station when a low-toned, raspy-voiced reporter informs his listeners that the president's deal with Iran for the production of nuclear reactors has passed, and sanctions will be lifted.

Rita jumps as the baby kicks in her womb, thrashing against his confines. She holds her stomach. He continues to thrash about as the news story continues, causing her to cry out in pain. Paul holds her as Francisco tries to console her. Realizing the connection, Paul asks Joey to turn off the radio.

Francisco realizes why the Messenger is being born at that time. Israel is gearing up for something big, ordering and receiving thirty-five of the United States' latest fighter jets, the best the world has ever seen. They have outfitted them with the highest technology and special instructions for short-flight missions. The jets will be Israel's most effective first line of defense, enough to stop Iran from wiping them off the face of the planet. The Antichrist has been unleashed on the world. Satan created him some thirty-four years earlier. Now he is a young, charismatic man who will become the president of Iran with the blessing of that country's highest leaders.

The Antichrist, the Beast, will become the instigator and agitator who will put a nuclearized Iran on a collision course with Israel. He will engineer a cataclysmic war, causing the unleashing of nuclear missiles on both countries. The missiles will trigger a domino effect from their respective allies, who are bound by religious, ideological, and political allegiances, all contributing to the annihilation of human life, unless the

Messenger's announcement of salvation is heard and received. He will become the Messenger of biblical scriptures and prophecy. He will warn humankind to ready themselves for the ultimate end. He will implore them to cleanse their souls and prepare for the Second Coming of Christ.

Satan cannot allow the Messenger to succeed. He must stop him from being born. Francisco knows he will use all his powers to extinguish him.

40

PEARLS BEFORE SWINE

When the white van passes the town of Cortland, New York, Rita starts feeling labor pains.

"How can this be?" she asks Paul. "The baby is only a few weeks old. I can't be going into labor."

Despite her doubts, her condition quickly becomes serious. Francisco asks Joey to pull off the highway to get to a hospital. Joey punches it into his GPS. The closest hospital is Cortland Regional Medical Center. He starts toward it.

Just then, Rita feels her water break. "What's going on?" she screams. "I can feel the baby coming out!"

"Joey, pull over, please!" Paul shouts.

Joey pulls over beside a pig farm.

"Oh, my God!" Rita screams. "The head is coming out! Lord, help me!"

Paul sees she is on the verge of hysteria. He places his hand over hers in hopes of calming her and asks everyone but Joey to get out of the van while he tends to her.

"I need some towels, Joey! And scissors!"

Joey brings aprons and towels used for his bakery, as well as a pair of scissors.

"I can see his head," Paul says as he attends to Rita. "Breathe, Rita! Push! Push!"

"Did you need to come back in my life?" she yells. "Why couldn't you leave me alone?" She tilts her head back in anguish. "Oh, my dear Lord! What's happening to me?"

With a final push, the baby is clear. Paul cuts the umbilical cord and pulls the afterbirth from her womb. Joey wraps the baby in towels and aprons.

Outside, the pigs start to become agitated. They gather in large numbers, staying close to one another, squealing. The sound gets louder until it reaches an unbearable pitch. Their eyes glow red in the night as the herd marches toward the fence. They surge against it and then break through, charging at the van.

The priests try slaughtering them with their knives, but there are too many.

"Get into the van!" Francisco yells.

As they run in front of the possessed pigs, one of the priests becomes overwhelmed and is brought down by the herd.

Paul jumps out of the van and splashes the herd with the blood from his wounds. As the blood hits the pigs, they squeal and retreat into the field. Some who receive a stronger dose of blood fall over dead.

Paul runs to where the priest fell. He splatters the pigs that surround him with the blood. They die instantly. Paul clears their carcasses away and discovers the priest's face has been bitten off, and his skull has been crushed open by the pigs' powerful jaws. His brain is completely eaten away.

"Paul, leave the Messenger Baby to the swine and go."

Paul looks up and sees that the voice—the dead priest's voice—is coming from a pig with the remains of the priest's brain dripping from its lips.

"Your lives will be spared. Do not end up like me. Francisco, you're going to die here. You can order Paul to leave the baby with us. That woman is a whore. She cannot bear the Messenger. Leave her and the baby here with us. We will take good care of them. You are going to be with me, Paul. You will give in to your desire of the flesh for your lovely Rita."

"Be gone from here, Satan!" Paul screams. Then he splashes a large amount of blood onto the pig, disintegrating him.

The dead priest is beyond help. Francisco kneels over the body and administers his last rites.

Meanwhile, the remaining pigs regroup. Their eyes glow bright red again as they charge at Francisco and Paul. Satan is furious that the Messenger has been born.

Paul forces Francisco back into the van as the other priests try to retrieve the body. Just as Francisco and Paul make it safely inside, the raging pigs attack. They ram the priests' legs like bulls, trying to knock them over and biting them to try to incapacitate them. The priests are forced to abandon the body of their fallen comrade and slash their way back to the van.

Paul jumps out of the van and thrashes his arm toward the possessed swine, but they don't retreat as quickly as before, dying where they stand or in mid-charge. Both priests are badly wounded as they stumble into the van.

Paul thumps on the side of the van. "Go! Go!"

Rita holds the baby as Francisco administers aid to his wounded priests. They leave the dead priest's body behind, and the pigs go into a feeding frenzy as they devour it.

Manny is heartbroken about losing a close friend, but he and the other priest are badly wounded. The other priest has lost three of his toes. They were bitten off, as was the front of his shoe. Paul managed to grab the part of his shoe with his toes still inside, hoping they can be reattached. They need medical help immediately. Joey has rerouted back toward the hospital.

Big Sonny has not moved from his seat, staying clear of the Catholic feud with the devil. "I don't understand this Catholic and devil stuff," he says. "All I can say is now I know why we Jews don't eat pigs. I'm just doing what I need to do to get you guys to Canada. Then you're on your own."

41

WOLVES AT THEIR DOOR

On the way to the hospital, Francisco decides to drop off Manny and the priest. He thinks it will be easier to get to Canada with fewer people, and the two priests can take care of each other. He orders them not to speak to anyone and to invoke diplomatic immunity and seek the protection of the Holy See.

They drop Manny off a block away, so the van won't be seen on the hospital's security cameras. Francisco blesses the two priests and assures them that he will see them back in Rome. Then Manny, with his arm around the wounded priest, heads toward the hospital holding the part of the priest's shoe with his toes inside.

Knowing that once the priests are discovered, the FBI will be on their trail, Francisco hopes that by then they will be already in Canada.

Tommaso has arranged for his Mafia contacts in Canada to be waiting on the American side of the border. He also gave Big Sonny the number of a road marker to turn off the I-87 about a mile from the border. There they will meet a couple of the Canadian Calabrian Mafia, better known as the 'Ndrangheta, a feared family that originated in Calabria, Italy. They will lead the way through thick brush and waterways into Canada, where a plane will be ready to take them to Rome.

After speaking with Tommaso, Sonny discards his cell phone and uses another one, so the FBI cannot track his signal.

Joey has been driving for better than four hours without saying much. As they enter the Adirondack Mountains in New York State, Joey feels something is wrong with the van. The temperature light turns on. He alerts his passengers of the problem and pulls off at the Schroon Lake exit.

Driving some two miles into town, he sees an old gas station with an auto repair sign. He pulls into the station, running over a hose that causes a ding to sound inside the station. "Man, I haven't seen a hose like that in years," he remarks.

Joey gets out and looks inside, thinking maybe they might get lucky and someone might be there, but the station is dark and devoid of life. He gets back in his van, in a hurry to leave, when he hears a faint voice.

"Yes, can I help you?"

Joey looks toward the voice but doesn't see anyone except for his van's white exhaust smoke billowing up into the night sky.

"Up here," the voice says.

Joe looks up at the second floor over the garage and sees a tall, old, portly man with an unkempt gray beard. He is wearing a baseball cap and a bright red checkered flannel shirt, his round belly protruding from his midsection. His face is pale, but his cheeks are red.

"I'll be right down," he says.

Moments later, he rounds the corner of the building. "How can I help you?"

"My engine light tells me I'm overheating," Joey says.

The old man puckers his lips and makes a hissing sound. "Hmm . . . this model is known for that."

Lifting the hood, he leans in and checks the engine. Then he steps back, shaking his head. "Just as I thought. Your radiator hose is broken."

"Can you fix it?" Joey asks.

"Sure can, but not today. I'll have to get the parts tomorrow morning. I don't have any in stock. There's a cabin rental place just down the road. I can call them and let them know you'll be coming by, if you like."

Joey confers with the others in the van, and they all agree the only thing to do is get a place to stay for the night. Rita is exhausted. She needs to rest, and the baby needs to be bathed.

The old man introduces himself as Kenny Flynn. They jump into his large pickup, which seats five comfortably, and drive into town, stopping at a twenty-four-hour supermarket to get supplies. Then they head for Ned's Cabin Rentals.

After checking in and settling down into a two-bedroom cabin, Rita falls fast asleep. The Messenger baby just looks around in silence, wrapped in a new blanket and guarded by Paul.

Francisco prepares food for everyone while Big Sonny and Joey sit on a sofa watching television. Suddenly, the lights flicker and then go out.

"Looks like a power failure, Father," Joey says.

Minutes later, they hear a knock on the cabin door. Everyone remains silent. The knock comes again, harder this time.

"Folks, it's Ned, the owner of this place. I brought a lantern for you."

Big Sonny nudges Joey. "You get it."

As Big Sonny stands behind the door, his hand concealed under his jacket, Joey opens the door and retrieves the lantern.

"Thank you," Joey says, smiling. "That's very thoughtful of you. God bless you."

"The power should be back on by daybreak," Ned says. "Sorry for the trouble." He hisses to himself and shakes his head. "These dang summer blackouts." Then he walks back toward his own cabin, a flashlight guiding his path.

Joey places the lantern in the middle of the table, and it illuminates the entire cabin, making it possible to move freely about. Francisco puts his cooking creation on the table, along with some dishes. He's combined tomato sauce and sausage with some pasta and served it all together in one dish. After he recites the Lord's Prayer and everyone makes the sign of the cross, they dig in.

As they eat, they hear howling in the distance. Adirondack wolves are thought to be extinct, although a few have been sighted in the area. A second wolf joins in.

"They must have smelled my cooking," Francisco jokes.

Laughter erupts from the group.

Outside, a thick white fog fills the cabin grounds, brought in by cold, gusting winds that blow fiercely from the lake. Large tree limbs adorned with thousands of leaves begin swaying and crashing against each other. The wolves' howling becomes louder as they approach, the winds also increasing in intensity.

The wolves are just below the window of where the Messenger baby is sleeping. Their howls become demonic in the tone.

Paul alerts Francisco that Satan's minions are near. "We must protect the baby!" They look at Rita. She is still sleeping, collapsed with exhaustion.

Francisco orders Big Sonny and Joey to barricade the windows with furniture. As they hurry to obey, they hear a loud crash, and a 200-pound white-and-gray wolf with a bushy tail smashes through an unprotected window. He is cut and bleeding from the shards of glass, but he is unfazed and determined. He looks around the room, but the Messenger baby is with Paul and Rita in the bedroom, and the door is locked.

Francisco lashes at the large animal with a knife, but the wolf retaliates, giving Francisco a vicious bite that rips open his forearm, from his elbow to his wrist.

Joey batters the wolf with a chair. Big Sonny brandishes his gun and shoots the beast right between the eyes, stopping the beast dead in his tracks.

Francisco is bleeding badly. Joey looks at his wound and then presses a towel over it. Almost immediately, the towel turns red with blood. "The cut is bad," Joey says. "We have to get to a hospital."

Francisco shakes his head, his face white. "No hospital."

Just then, they hear another crash in the bedroom.

42

ON THE ROAD AGAIN

An even larger wolf stands in the middle of the bedroom, growling. Rita screams as the vicious beast advances toward Paul, who stands in front of her and the baby. His shouts for the animal to leave have no effect. Paul glances at the door. There's no way he and Rita can make it there with the baby. Guessing Paul's intention, the beast blocks their path, snarling and making bluff charges at them.

In the main room, Big Sonny and Joey pound on the door, kicking it and smashing their bodies against it, but the door won't break. Then Joey gets an idea. "Sonny, give me your gun!"

Paul lands a kick into the beast's side. Rita grabs the baby and wraps him in a protective mother's hold, willing to sacrifice herself to save his life. The kick temporarily stops the possessed beast. As Paul tries to unleash the stigmata blood, the beast lunges at him and pins him to the floor, Paul's arm inside the wolf's mouth.

Paul feels the canine's powerful jaws and large teeth rip into his flesh. He screams in pain. "Rita, take the baby and run!"

She can't move, frozen in fear.

Badly wounded, Paul sticks his thumb into the wolf's eye, causing the beast to release his grip. As Paul struggles to his feet, the wolf turns to face Rita and the baby, saliva and blood dripping from its horrible jaws.

Outside, Joey tries to reach the bedroom window, but it's too high. "Here's the gun!" he screams. "Shoot it!" He throws the gun through the window, not knowing where it will land.

Rita, who is backing away, lands in a sitting position with the baby in her arms in front of her. She thrusts herself backward in her effort to get away from the wolf and lands right on top of the gun. The wolf approaches slowly, pulling back its top lip, revealing its large canine teeth. It growls and swipes at her face, just missing her. She shakes with fear, pinned against the wall with nowhere to run. Then she feels for the gun beneath her.

Just as the wolf opens its mouth and lunges forward, Rita sticks her hand in the beast's mouth, the gun firmly in her grasp.

"No!" she screams, and then pulls the trigger.

The top of the wolf's head explodes, spraying brain matter, blood, and teeth throughout the room. The wolf's large body falls over, dead, the threat extinguished.

Rita opens the bedroom door, and Big Sonny and Joey administer aid to Paul and Francisco. They realize they must leave the area. Luckily for them, Ned has the same van as Joey. They leave three hundred dollars on the front seat of Ned's van, steal his radiator hose, walk over to the garage, where Joey's van is waiting to be fixed, and install it themselves. Then they drive back to the cabin to pick up the others and get back on the I-87, headed toward Canada.

Driving on the road, they see the road marker where Tomas told them to turn off. Big Sonny is on the phone with his counterparts from the Canadian side telling them they are almost there.

As they turn off the road, and the pavement turns to gravel, they see a flashlight waving slowly up and down. It is Luigi and Cesare, two Italian Mafia soldiers from Canada.

Both men are eager to get moving before daylight. Big Sonny and Joey help Francisco and Paul into Luigi and Cesare's vehicle. Rita walks on her own, refusing to let go of the baby.

Francisco and Paul thank Big Sonny and Joey for their help. Francisco gives Joey a ring. "Joey, you will always be in my prayers."

Joey bows his head. "Thank you, Father."

They hug, and then the torch is passed.

Luigi and Cesare are two fast-moving men who drive with a fury, trying to sneak into Canada under the cover of night, but daylight arrives before they reach their destination.

Reverting to their backup plan, they change direction and drive for just over an hour. As the ground gets softer and the passengers see large weeds parting as they drive through them, Luigi looks back at Francisco and speaks in Italian. Both Paul and Francisco are fluent. "It will take a few more minutes to get to Lake Champlain in Vermont. From there, we'll get into Canada by boat." He says they know the shipping route well. It is their main means of making a living as smugglers.

They come to a sudden stop just off the marshlands near Lake Champlain outside of Burlington, Vermont. Luigi and Cesare say they will have to walk in some muddy water to reach the boat. Their plan is to sneak into Canada under the guise of recreational boaters.

Daylight is already upon them as they follow Luigi into the vast marshlands, Cesare bringing up the rear to make sure no one steps off the path. One step in either direction could cause them to fall into twelve feet of water. The pathway was made possible by the two men's ingenuity. They painstakingly excavated the marshlands a little at a time and built a winding walkway that sometimes has them walking in circles in ankle-deep water. It is designed to throw any law enforcement off their scent. Luigi and Cesare spent three years making the walkway undetectable. They also built a hidden dock with a berth deep enough for their boat. The dock is disguised as a tree that drifted into the marshlands, but it is cemented to the bottom. They made the undetectable dock in the middle of the marsh, so their boat cannot be seen.

Their efforts have served them well. Both men have made small fortunes avoiding the authorities and eluding customs in either direction. Their enterprise has kept the Royal Canadian Mounted Police (RCMP) baffled for years.

As the group walks farther into the marshes, Cesare and Luigi's boat appears through the thinning weeds. It's a forty-two-foot Sea Ray sedan bridge powerboat built in 2005. It is a workhorse, and it has enough power to move large amounts of whatever product they choose to smuggle. Nondescript, it blends in easily with the other boats on the lake.

Luigi helps Rita and the baby on board. Getting Francisco on the boat proves a bit harder. Paul, Cesare, and Luigi join forces, lifting him on board. Paul climbs in behind him. Then Cesare unties the boat from the tree, arches his body, and thrusts himself forward as he pushes the boat's bow, easily pulling himself on deck. Once on board, he walks up the steps to the upper deck to join Luigi.

The boat glides through the water for a short distance. Then black exhaust erupts from the stern as a cranking sound comes from the boat's engine. It fires up like a fine-tuned machine. Luigi pushes forward on the throttle, and they are on their way to Canada.

43

Not Quite Tourists

Back in Schroon Lake, following the wolf attack, Ned calls the local authorities, who alert the FBI. The feds arrive on the scene and enter the cabin, which looks like a satanic ritual gone horrifically wrong.

With the two priests in custody, claiming diplomatic immunity and refusing to talk, the FBI also pick up Joey and Big Sonny along the I-87. They were heading southbound toward New York. Neither the two men nor the two priests are helpful to the FBI's investigation, frustrating the agent in charge.

Onboard the boat, Paul and Francisco enjoy a shower and a change of clothing, courtesy of the smugglers. The clothes are part of the smugglers' last load, which was shipped into the United States. It includes suits, shirts, shoes, and beautifully tailored women's clothing. They transport the stolen merchandise to Harold the Haberdasher, a wholesale distributor of fine clothing on the New York side of the border. Their price is always very reasonable. Harold has salesmen waiting all over New York to receive their merchandise. It is a lucrative arrangement for Harold, who has become a well-known dealer in fine Canadian clothing and is sought after for his wares.

Heading up Lake Champlain toward Burlington, Vermont is a routine trip for Luigi and Cesare. Burlington is a small lakefront tourist town. Docking their boat at the marina, the group makes their way into town.

Burlington is a bustling place with attractions and rides, restaurants, small shops that give the town a warm, welcoming feeling, as if it were a town fair. The group buys all kinds of goods and medical supplies. Luigi and Cesare pay for everything, out of respect for Tommaso.

The group sits down in an outdoor café and orders some espresso and sodas and some small pastries. As the men talk. Rita plays with the baby, which has already grown to the size of an eight-month-old. They just bought new clothes for the baby, but he will outgrow them soon. Rita is not alarmed, knowing the baby is a special child.

Luigi looks across the street and notices an older, frail-looking man trying to act incognito. He feels the man watching them, but he doesn't look like law enforcement. Is he imagining things? He's not sure why the old man would be interested in the group, but he certainly is.

Luigi nudges Cesare, who is talking to Francisco, and tilts his head toward the man across the street. Cesare also picks up on the man's interest in their group. He motions for Luigi to take a closer look.

Luigi gets up, concealing himself in the crowd, and positions himself half a block away, inside a t-shirt shop. He watches the man pretending to read a newspaper, pausing occasionally to peer over the top of it at the group.

Luigi looks around but doesn't see anyone else behaving suspiciously. The old man seems to be alone, his baseball cap pulled down low, concealing his face. Luigi thinks the man is too old to be law enforcement. He leans more toward him simply being crazy rather than a threat.

He makes his way back to the café and rejoins the group. Cesare looks at Luigi, and Luigi shakes his head, indicating the old man is nothing to worry about.

A few minutes later, the group is headed back to the marina when Luigi looks up and yells, "Look out!"

One of the large sailboats' masts is falling right toward the group. Cesare opens his arms wide and pushes them all forward. The mast smashes right through the dock behind them with a terrible splintering noise.

People in the area gasp and scream in fear. Luigi jumps over the gap in the dock and joins the group. Then they all hurry onto the boat and make their way out of the marina.

Looking back at the dock, Luigi sees the older man with the baseball cap staring at them from the sailboat where the mast came crashing down. Luigi nudges Cesare and points at him. A strange feeling fills both men.

Francisco realizes Satan is on a mission to kill the Messenger baby and will stop at nothing. He must get the baby inside the walls of the Vatican as soon as possible. It is the only place where he will be safe.

As the boat motors toward Canada, Francisco calls the cardinal who oversees Quebec, Cardinal Pierre Pardo. He smiles when he hears the cardinal's voice. "Hello, Pierre. This is Francisco Libatore."

Pierre, who is also a Jesuit, is overjoyed at hearing from the head of the Jesuit Order. "How are you, Superior General? So good to hear your voice."

"Wonderful to hear yours as well, Cardinal," Francisco replies. "I need your help."

"Yes, of course, Superior General. Whatever you need."

Francisco quickly explains what they will need when they reach Quebec.

"I'm not sure if I have the authority or the power to do what you are asking of me, Francisco, but I will do anything to oblige my Superior General. I will use all my power to get this done for you. I am sure you know this."

"Yes, of course, Cardinal Pardo. Can you please call the Holy Father and give him this code?" He relays a succession of numbers, a code requesting immediate assistance from the Pope. Francisco knows this will unleash the Vatican's power and put in motion the resources he requires.

44

A BATTLE IN QUEBEC

The FBI, who is tracking the group's whereabouts, picks up the telephone conversation via satellite surveillance. The State Department officials stationed at the US embassy in Quebec are ordered to execute the FBI's plan. FBI agents and State Department officials stationed at the embassy arrange to intercept the group at the docks, rescue Rita, and arrest her captors.

Meanwhile, the Pope has directed Cardinal Pardo to the meeting with the premier of Quebec and the director general of the Quebec Provincial Police (QPP), both of whom have already spoken with the Pope. The cardinal claims that Paul and Francisco are protected by diplomatic immunity and are to be treated as such.

As the boat pulls up to the dock, a slough of FBI agents and State Department officials are waiting. Cardinal Pardo is also there, accompanied by fifty members of his congregation, as are forty officers from the QPP and the QPP's assistant deputy director, François De Klerk, who represents the government of Canada. He takes his orders from the general director of the QPP.

An argument over who has jurisdictional powers ensues. The United States ambassador, the FBI, and the State Department officials are adamant that they have full jurisdictional rights over Rita, a US citizen. The QPP officers and the FBI agents get into a shoving match as Cardinal Pardo and his flock form a protective wall for Francisco and Paul. The State Department in Washington is on the phone with the ambassador.

Two helicopters from the Canadian coast guard hover over the melee. Cardinal Pardo and his followers quickly descend upon the docks. De Klerk approaches the cardinal.

"We can't just let the woman go with them," De Klerk says. "We must interview her to determine if she is being held against her will. If that is, in fact, what is happening, then we will have to detain the two Vatican officials. I want to make this very clear. We are not arresting them, merely detaining them."

More church members arrive at what is fast becoming an international incident. The American ambassador is insisting on taking Rita with him to the American embassy, where the interview can be conducted, but De Klerk refuses to allow it. "We will take her to police headquarters and do a full investigation there."

"No, I don't think so!" the ambassador shouts.

His loud, condescending tone angers De Klerk. "This is Canada," he says with a high-pitched voice in a distinctly French accent. "You are in our country, and we have jurisdiction. We call the fucking shots, not you."

The ambassador shoots him a look like he has just eaten a rotten egg, pointing his finger at De Klerk's face. "It seems like you don't like your job very much, director. Keep talking to me like that, and you will be demoted to street cleaner."

De Klerk loses his composure and grabs the ambassador by the lapels. "Are you threatening me? Who the fuck do you think you're talking to? I'm an official with the Canadian government. You're just a guest here."

Pandemonium erupts on the docks as the QPP, the FBI, and the State Department officials try to break up the fight between De Klerk and the ambassador.

Cardinal Pardo smiles when he sees Francisco. "Welcome to Quebec, Superior General." He greets him and Paul with a hug.

Francisco points at all the ruckus on the docks. "I see you've done a good job."

Pardo smiles. "It's the least I can do for my Superior General." "Pierre, can you get us to one of our churches quickly before calm is restored?" Francisco asks, eager to take advantage of the distraction. His plan is to have the Canadian police do a quick investigation, only in familiar surroundings.

Two blocks away is the amazing church of Notre Dame de Quebec. Paul, Francisco, Rita, and the baby are taken there by limousine. An alert QPP officer sees them fleeing and gives chase in his cruiser.

The limousine passes through the open wrought-iron gate that leads into the church courtyard, the gates shutting quickly behind it, preventing the police from entering.

A friar stands in front of the gate. The policeman demands he open it, but the friar calmly refuses, citing diplomatic immunity. The police-man radios De Klerk, and soon he and the American ambassador are there with their people. They gather outside of the church's gate demanding to speak to Rita.

The friar walks out and informs De Klerk that an interview will be conducted inside the church. Both De Klerk and the American ambassador are allowed in. The friar leads them through the magnificent church. They walk through a maze of corridors, eventually arriving at the church's large office, where Rita, Paul, Francisco, and Cardinal Pardo are seated.

The ambassador begins the interview by speaking directly to Rita. "I am the ambassador for the United States. My name is Archibald Smith, but you can call me Archie, like the comic book." He uses humor in an attempt to help Rita relax. "I am here to take you home. All you have to do is tell me what you want. I promise you with all the power of the United States government that you will be able to leave here with me, and you will be home before the evening news." He shoots a look at De Klerk. "No one will stop you. It's your right as an American citizen."

De Klerk looks at the ambassador and mouths two words: "Fuck you."

Rita remains silent.

"If you are being held against your will, please tell us," De Klerk says, "and we will help you."

Rita maintains her silence. Stares are thrown all over the room as those in authority try to figure out what to do. Finally, Rita looks up. "I was never held against my will. I chose to be with the man I love. Now I am in love with my Lord and Savior. I am sorry, but I will not go with you. God has a plan for me, and I am going to follow it. I will be staying here. I have been treated well, and I am in fine health. Please relay that to my family back home. Actually, I am doing remarkably well."

Ambassador Smith is not convinced. "They have brainwashed you," he says. "You aren't thinking clearly. I'm going to walk out those gates with you. You will be back in the States tonight with your family." He stands up and holds out his hand. "Rita, come with me."

Rita smiles politely. "I'm sorry, but I have to refuse. Truly, it is my wish to remain here. Please, don't take this the wrong way. I love my country and my family back home; that will never change. But I have a calling, a true purpose, and I must go where it leads me. That's all I have to say. Thank you so much, Mr. Ambassador, for all your concern and help, but I must obey God's will."

Francisco raises his eyes at Paul and Cardinal Pardo as if to say, "That went rather well, don't you think?"

Realizing she is not leaving, Ambassador Smith walks out to his waiting contingent, feeling dejected and disappointed, and relays what happened inside. De Klerk does the same.

Outside the church, the QPP have posted two police cars to make sure there are no unwanted SWAT-type rescue operations from the American embassy.

45

HOME SWEET ROME

Paul and Francisco make plans to get to the airport in the morning. The Pope has arranged for one of Canada's richest men, who is also a devout Catholic, to donate his private jet to transport Paul, Francisco, Rita, and the Messenger baby to Rome.

The group rests for the night inside the church's guest quarters. While the others sleep, Paul sits guard outside of Rita and the baby's room. Falling in and out of a light sleep, he wakes up every few minutes and peeks in on Rita and Elijah.

While dozing, he hears a strange sound coming from their room. He tries to open the door, but it is locked. Surging with adrenaline, he smashes against the door, and it flies open.

Inside, he sees the tall elderly man with the baseball cap from back in Burlington. Having climbed in through the window, he is holding a large hunting knife. Paul stands in front of Messenger baby, so the man grabs Rita out of bed, yanks her head back by her hair, and holds his knife to her throat. He draws blood as the large hunting knife's teeth tear into her skin.

"Kill him, Paul!" the old man screams. "Kill him, or I'll kill your Rita!"

She flinches as she feels the warm lines of blood run down her neck, the knife's teeth digging deeper into her skin. "No, let him live!" she cries, struggling to break free, but the old man has incredible strength despite his years.

"Last chance, Paul!" the old man shouts. "Kill him now!"

When Paul still refuses to obey, the old man nods. "Okay, Paul, Rita dies."

He moves his knife to sever her carotid artery, which will ensure her quick death. But before he can, Paul, using his gift of bilocation, is instantaneously across the room. He yanks on the man's arm, pulling it away from Rita's neck.

Paul struggles with the man, but he slithers out of Paul's grasp and runs to the open window. He climbs out and slides down the side of the building, jumping off halfway down and running into the darkness.

After binding the superficial wounds on Rita's neck, Paul stays awake all night waiting for the intruder to return, but he never does.

Early the next morning, Cardinal Pardo drives them to the airport. A caravan of police cars follows, making sure nothing happens to them while in Quebec. The premier is extremely sensitive about avoiding an international incident.

When they arrive at Quebec international airport, a police escort leads them onto the runway, and they hurry aboard their plane. Francisco pauses at the top of the steps and waves goodbye to De Klerk, who bids them a fond farewell, relieved they are finally off his hands.

Soon, they are cleared for takeoff. Everyone relaxes as the plane's wheels leave the ground.

Rita plays with the ever-growing baby as Francisco talks with Paul. "How long do you think we have before the Messenger baby completes its mission?" Francisco asks.

Paul looks at the baby and shrugs. "I don't know exactly, but the way he's growing, it won't be long."

Francisco looks back to check on the baby's rapid growth. He knows the answer to the question he is about to ask, but he hopes to hear something different. "Paul, is his mission to announce the end of times?"

Paul looks at Francisco as he would look at his own father if he were coming to terms with his own mortality. "Francisco, you know the answer to that question."

Nodding sadly, Francisco turns away and stares out at the vastness of the sky, consumed by his thoughts.

Hours later, the plane lands safely at Rome's international airport. A limousine is waiting for them on the tarmac. They are whisked away to the Vatican, where the Pope is anxious to meet the Messenger baby, hoping many of his questions will be answered.

As soon as the Messenger baby sees the Pope, the child's face lights up, and he reaches for him. Smiling, the Pope takes the baby in his arms. Immediately, he is overcome by an intense feeling unlike anything he has experienced before, a deep, resounding sensation of love and warmth that causes him to stagger. Concerned, the priests reach out to support him, but he waves them away. He realizes the feeling is a message sent directly from God. The feeling resonates deep within him, wave after wave of euphoria rippling through him. His mind is clear, and he knows without a doubt that the baby's spirit came directly from God.

"This baby is holy and is truly sent from the house of the Lord," the Pope proclaims. He lifts the baby above his head. "It is your will, Lord, that the Messenger will dwell here in your house on Earth. It is so ordered by the powers vested in me by the Father."

The Pope lowers the baby, his mind already beginning to process the reality of the world's end.

46

THE RISE OF THE BEAST

While campaigning for the presidency of Iran at a gathering called for by the Ayatollah, the supreme leader of Iran, the Beast wins over the power elites and the supreme leader. He charms and sways them toward him with his words.

When it is his turn to give his speech, the Beast stands silently at the podium, staring straight ahead above the audience's heads. He waits until all chatter stops, and an inquisitive silence fills the room. All eyes are fixed on him and his Hollywood looks. His deep blue eyes stand out against his olive skin. He looks fresh and healthy, with thick, shiny, neatly groomed black hair parted on the side. His face is young and chiseled, and his features are perfectly proportioned, his dimpled cheeks adding a boyish handsomeness. He is tall and slender and is fitted in a masterfully tailored suit made from the finest material. His tie is perfectly fitted into the collar of his tailored shirt.

Once he is certain he has everyone's undivided attention, he breaks his silence, his voice aflame with fiery passion. "Israel is not our enemy but our friend."

Sounds of dismay fill the room, and heads shake. The Ayatollah's guards glance toward him, awaiting his instructions. He is aware of their apprehension, but he squints and shakes his head. He wants to hear more of what the young man has to say. Tensions are lowered for the moment.

"The sworn enemy of Iran should be the cause of our own indecision and lack of resolve for not taking the necessary steps to engage Israel and the United States," the Beast continues. "In the same way, they threaten to engage us. The only way to eliminate that threat is to be a nuclear power, and as many deterrents as they have facing us, we must have facing them."

A blast of cheers and clapping erupts.

He continues from within a trance of pure conviction and authority. "We must be honest with ourselves and proceed with fierce determination. Why do we let the infidels invade our lands, kill our brothers and sisters, and dictate our role and our future in our region? Brothers, the task is clear. We must be the leader, for our reason to be the leader is the truest of all. If not us, then there is no one. We will lead the region and rid this curse that has been thrust upon us. We will be the catalyst to unite the entire Middle East."

He pauses as more cheers and applause erupt.

"Our mission is not an easy one. But when has anything ever been easy for Iran? We must relish our role, and we must be resolute, stopping at nothing to end the violence that divides our region. We must set our differences aside and join forces with our neighbors."

Inquisitive looks are exchanged around the room, with many looking at the Ayatollah to gauge his reaction.

"Do you ask yourself, 'Why Iran?'" Lifting his fist into the air, he pouts with anger and then falls silent before continuing in a low tone. "The reason is clear. Because it is so demanded by our Creator! Iran must be the unifier, the protector, and the leader. It is time to fulfill what our Creator demands of us. We must free our region and rid it of Israel and the influence of the great Satan, the United States! Only Iran can achieve its rightful greatness and our rightful position as the world's greatest leader. May the Creator bless us and guide us on our mission toward greatness."

The Ayatollah nods in agreement, showing his pleasure and solidarity with the Beast's vision for Iran.

Upon seeing the Ayatollah's reaction, all in attendance leap to their feet with cheers and applause. The Beast steps away from the podium, bows to the Ayatollah, and places his hand over his heart.

The hand-picked successor originally slated to win the presidency looks around the large auditorium. He is filled with concern, his solid path to the presidency in ruins.

The Beast, a.k.a. Dr. Ali Gilani, a PhD in political science who holds a professorship at Iran's leading university, has tapped the people's hearts with his words. As Satan's creation, he receives his orders directly from Satan himself. Like his Satanic father, Gilani is dignified, handsome, charismatic, amazingly intelligent, extremely charming, and has a wicked wit.

Satan has created an amazing cover for his creation and has placed him right in the middle of the most troubled part of the world. It was all planned precisely so Gilani could assume power as soon as the American president agreed to Iran's nuclear ambitions. Now Iran is racing to complete its ultimate goal: offensive nuclear weapons of mass destruction. Iran knows the world is watching, so it must tread carefully or risk a preemptive attack from the United States and Israel. Once Iran has a nuclear arsenal, it is much less likely that their enemies will attack, their arsenal acting as a deterrent. They are less than two years away from achieving their goal. By then, Iran will be fully capability of attaching nuclear warheads to rockets capable of reaching the United States and Israel. When Gilani takes his place as president of Iran, he will accelerate the process to only eighteen months. Soon, the world will be on the brink of self-annihilation.

All this will cause the Messenger to begin his mission on Earth at the exact age of thirty-three. He will tell the world to ready itself for the Second Coming of the Messiah. His return is at hand.

47

THE RETURN OF ARTURO

Arturo Spennili is a well-built man of medium height with salt-and-pepper hair that is always cut short. His face is full and round. His body fits well into designer sweat suits, which has become his signature dress.

Arturo heard rumors while in jail that upset him. He was told that when Tamasso retires or passes his position on, it will go to Johnny rather then him. By all accounts, Arturo was the heir apparent. He is, in street terms, a true stand-up guy and a brutal gangster, but the older gangsters consider him to be all balls and guts and no brains. Tomas used him strictly for his brutality. Arturo went to jail for witnessing a policemen's murder and not telling the police what he saw. He was true to the code of silence by which all stand-up gangsters live by. When he was asked repeatedly, he kept saying he did not know and had not seen anything. The police were not having any of it. They beat him to a pulp and then charged him with the murder. The false charges stuck, and he was sentenced to seventeen years in state prison. Now his time is up, and he is being released.

He had shown his loyalty to Tomas on numerous occasions before he went to prison. A young man was robbing stores in the neighborhood and was seen by local residents. The storeowners complained and asked for help from Tomas, who always kept the neighborhood safe and free of crime, seeing as it was his neighborhood. He sent for the young man who was seen committing the crimes.

Eddie, a.k.a. Eddie "Boots" Calandra, was a thin but strong and wiry man whose reddish hair and rugged freckled face made him an anomaly in the neighborhood. He got the name "Boots," because he always wore leather boots of some kind. He had a quick temper and was fast to administer swift and harsh punishment with his hands. His amazing fighting abilities were well known.

When Boots showed up to see Tommaso in his restaurant, he was instructed to wait in a hallway in the building next door. As soon as Tomas entered the building, he started yelling at Eddie. "You're robbing in my neighborhood!" Before Boots could answer, Tomas smashed the young man across his face.

It took all Boots's strength to restrain himself. "Tomas, don't do that again."

Tomas looked at him, puzzled. "What did you say?" Boots knew it meant certain death to hit a made member, especially one as high ranking as Tomas. Tomas approached him and repeated his question. "What did you just say?" Then he slapped Boots even harder.

Unable to restrain himself, Boots pummeled Tommaso, dropping him to the floor. It was a death sentence, brought upon himself by his own hands.

After leaving and cooling down, he realized what he had done. He summoned his partner in crime, Lorenzo "Teddy Bear" Certo. Teddy Bear was a gentle heavy-set man whose body resembled a large teddy bear. His floppy, curly locks surrounded his face, making him look like a cartoon character, and his animated expressions were docile, giving him a harmless and gentle presence. When Boots explained what had happened, Teddy Bear couldn't believe his ears.

"What happened? Can you run that by me again?" After Boots repeated his story, Teddy Bear looked at the ground and shook his head. "This is bad. It's worse than bad. You better get the fuck out of here and go to Siberia."

Boots responded with a lazy jerk of his shoulders and a slant of his head. "Fuck it. If they kill me, they kill me."

That they will, my friend, Teddy Bear thought. *That they will.*

Teddy Bear walked home after leaving Eddie Boots. When he arrived at his building, he noticed the lights in his hallway were off. He assumed one of the circuit breakers must have tripped, causing a power outage. The moment he entered his hallway, he was struck in the head by a baseball bat. He fell to his knees. Then someone shoved a hard, cold rounded piece of steel into his mouth, knocking out two of his bottom teeth.

"Hi, Teddy Bear. Where's your friend, Boots?"

"Take the gun out of my mouth," Teddy Bear mumbled.

His assailant slowly complied. His mouth swelling, Teddy Bear spit out a mouthful of blood. "Why are you doing this to me?"

He was answered by another vicious blow to the head, knocking him to the floor. Lying on his back and holding his head, he looked up at his assailant, Arturo, who pressed the gun to the side of Teddy Bear's head. "Listen, you motherfucker, you're going to call Boots, and you're going to tell him to meet you in the alley behind this building tomorrow at twelve o'clock, and then you're going to disappear from this neighborhood forever. You understand me?" He pressed the gun harder into the side of Teddy Bear's head.

Teddy bear knew of Arturo's ruthless reputation. He held up his hands in compliance. "Yes, okay."

"You tell him you have hot merchandise to show him. You got that?"

"Yes, okay, Arturo, I will."

48

THE CLOCK STRIKES TWELVE

Boots walked into an alley leading into a concrete yard that separated the two buildings. He entered a door that was used for storage in the building's basement. The room was lit by a small window that let daylight through.

"Teddy Bear," he called.

He was answered by a voice that Boots did not want to hear. "I have the hot merchandise." Arturo appeared out of a dark shadow in the corner of the cold basement.

Boots knew his most trusted friend had set him up. A sinking feeling of dread overwhelmed his body, and his limbs became heavy. Arturo was an ex-boxer and fifty pounds heavier, not to mention more vicious than Eddie. Eddie knew Arturo was not there to have a boxing match or a fair fight. He thought of running, but then he heard one of Arturo's associates locking the door. He was stuck like a fly on flypaper.

Arturo raised a gun and pointed it at Boots. "You knew we would come for you. Why did you stay?"

"Tomas was like a father to me. I just reacted to the physical contact. After I did it, I was sorry. I know I did the wrong thing. I thought we could talk about it, and it would be straightened out. My uncle, my mother's brother, will stand up for me. You would be making a big mistake if you did anything here without talking to him."

Arturo stared at Boots with a look of sarcastic bewilderment. "Your uncle gave the all-clear, and we are good to go."

In a last-ditch effort to save himself, Boots lunged at Arturo. He managed to get two steps toward him before he felt a burning-hot bullet enter his thigh and shatter his femur, causing him to fall to the cold basement floor. Bleeding, he looked up at Arturo. "Finish it."

Arturo answered coldly by pulling the trigger three more times.

Boots was found the next day. The message was well received, and order was fiercely restored and maintained.

49

MIKEY, "HOT DOG," THE ANGEL

A welcome home party is held for Arturo in Tomas's restaurant on Arthur Avenue. At the party are all those who are associated with Tomas and Arturo's family. A band with a local Italian crooner, Johnny Sal, is playing in the large room at the back of the restaurant that is used for parties. All the dishes Arturo enjoyed before he went away are on the table: chicken Scarpariello with sausage and potatoes, chicken cacciatore, fusilli pasta with peas in a red tomato sauce, veal with a white sauce with potatoes, broccoli rabe, Italian bread from his favorite bakery, fresh fish from Cosenza's fish store, and Italian cold cuts and cheese platters from the Title brothers' Italian deli, owned and operated by a Jewish family. Their deli has been part of the Italian neighborhood for over 100 years. It has been passed down from generation to generation. They speak Italian as well as any Italian immigrants and are pillars of the neighborhood to this very day. The Title brothers proudly display the Star of David on the front step of their store. Gil Title and his son, Gilbert, are guests at the party.

As Arturo enters, he is besieged with well-wishers, who give him kisses and hugs and envelopes filled with cash to help him get back on his feet. It is customary for people who just got out of prison to receive such gifts.

Tomas looks around the room and does not see Johnny. He remembers he forgot to invite him. He motions for a local young man who knows the neighborhood and its ways. His name is Mike, a.k.a. Hot Dog, a charismatic man who is beloved by the neighborhood. He truly had no enemies. Tomas describes him as an angel.

Johnny has known Hot Dog since he was a young boy. Tomas picked him for that reason. Both men have a genuine love, respect, and admiration for each other. Mike looks up to Johnny like an older brother. He visited Johnny in jail often and sent him food packages of Italian delicacies, pastry, and books. There is a true bond between them. Tomas knows Hot Dog can get Johnny to come to the party.

Hot Dog rings Johnny's doorbell, and Johnny opens the door. It's the first time he's seen Hot Dog since he's been home. "Hot Dog!" Johnny exclaims, and they hug each other. "How have you been, Hot Dog? Good to see you."

"I never thought I'd get to see you on the outside again," Hot Dog replies. "Great to see you home, Johnny." After the initial shock of seeing Johnny subsides, Hot Dog continues. "I'm doing great, but I'm getting a bit tired of seeing the same faces every day."

Johnny looks at Hot Dog trough nostalgic eyes, remembering him as a young boy when he operated amusement stands in the local Italian feasts. Hot Dog would come to his basketball stand and win constantly, cleaning Johnny out of all his stuffed animal prizes, until Johnny wouldn't let him play anymore. He reminds Hot Dog of the incident, and they both laugh. Johnny is happy to see Hot Dog again. Hot Dog knows Johnny's funny bone. He knows how to uses his quick wit and charm to get around him.

"Mike, come in, have something to eat."

Hot Dog responds with a comical sigh. "Another time, son. I'll have to take a rain check."

Johnny shakes his head, chuckling. "Sure, anytime."

"Johnny, Tomas is throwing a welcome home party for Arturo, and he wants you to come by."

Johnny's eyes widen in surprise. "Arturo got out? When?"

"Yesterday."

"Good to hear. Send him my regards. I would come by, but I'm a little tied up right now."

Hot Dog smiles. "Come on, John." He grins comically, changing his voice to drag out his words. "You know you're talking to me now, John." He grins in exaggerated disbelief, causing Johnny to laugh.

Johnny can't say no to Hot Dog's charm, wit, and humor. Still smiling, Johnny gives in. "Okay, okay, let me get dressed. I'll be right down."

Hot Dog and Johnny enter the party through a private entrance. Upon seeing Johnny, the crowd stares as if an A-list celebrity had just walked into the room. Whispers and murmurs fill the air. "Look, it's Johnny Ciminetti."

Johnny's presence steals the thunder from Arturo at his own party. The look on Arturo's face says it all. He fumes, consumed with anger. This world isn't big enough for the two of us, he concludes. The devil is using his tools of jealousy and vanity. Arturo will soon make his move on Johnny as the devil stays close by his side to guide him.

The next morning, Hot Dog comes by Johnny's house wearing white denim jeans, sneakers, and an open-collared shirt. Hot Dog has a full head of dark blond hair that is neatly combed back. He is a handsome young man, just above average height, and his workouts afford him a wiry and muscular frame. He beeps his horn, and Johnny comes out and gets in Hot Dog's dark-red Monte Carlo.

Parking on 187th Street and Cambreleng Avenue, when they get out, they run straight into Father Paul, who is walking on 187th Street. Hot Dog, a parishioner at Mt. Carmel, knows Father Paul from church. "Hey, Father Paul, do you want to have coffee with us?"

Paul smiles warmly. "Sure, I'd love a cup."

Johnny is perturbed by Paul's presence. He knows Big Sonny and Joey helped get Paul out of the country at great risk to themselves. Johnny had to ask Tomas for a large favor to do it.

"Why did you come back here after you got away?" Johnny asks. He shakes his head. "I mean, do you want to get caught?"

They walk into Joseph Calavolpe's pastry shop on 187th Street and Crescent Avenue. After passing the display of fine Italian pasty and birthday cakes, they sit at a round table.

"Well, I just got here," Paul says.

Hot Dog orders espressos and cannoli and some sweet Italian cookies for all.

Outside, police officers involved in the search for Paul and the Father General spot Paul and get in position to arrest him.

Feeling betrayed, Johnny repeats his question. "Why did you come back here?"

Paul smiles slightly. "I'm here on a saving mission."

Johnny becomes agitated by Paul's answer. He knows his chance of getting caught are 100 percent, seeing as the police are combing the streets for him. After all Johnny has done to keep Paul safe, Johnny's face bursts with anger. "What saving mission?"

Paul pulls up his sleeves. "This one." He exposes his wounds. Immediately, a large fine mist of blood forms around Hot Dog and Johnny. Just then, bullets fly, and the sound of gunshots fill the air. Arturo has entered through a side door and opened fire with a .45-caliber pistol in each hand, shooting round after round at Hot Dog and Johnny. The bullets are stopped in midair by the fine mist of blood. A total of nine bullets are suspended in the air right before they would have entered each man's body. Shocked and bewildered, Arturo flees the scene.

Johnny and Hot dog are stunned. Hot Dog turns to Johnny and clears his throat. "Did that fucking Arturo just try and kill us?"

The bullets fall to the floor as the fine mist dissipates. Johnny and Hot Dog turn to Paul. He smiles at both men and then disappears. Paul has used his gift of bi-location to save Paul and Hot Dog.

"Wait a second," Hot Dog says, still trying to understand, "what just happened? Did I miss something?" In response, Joey looks up to the heavens and makes the sign of the cross.

While leaving the pastry shop, Arturo is intercepted by the two police officers who were there to arrest Paul. Hot Dog and Johnny watch from the large glass window. Arturo turns quickly and fires a final round at Johnny. The bullet rips through the glass. Luckily for Johnny, Hot Dog sees Arturo's intention and instinctively shoves Johnny to the side. Arturo's bullet narrowly misses its intended target. Arturo turns his gun on the police officers as he takes shelter behind a delivery truck. The police return fire, and Arturo is hit multiple times and killed. Johnny is now clearly the heir apparent to Tommaso's throne.

50

DEEP QUESTIONS

Soon after arriving at the Vatican, Elijah, the Messenger, comes to resemble a seventeen-year-old boy. He is a tall, slim, serious young man with a medium build and dark hair that falls around his face. He is astute and always in observation mode, focused on his mission. He spends all his time with Francisco, Paul, and Rita, who has become a nun, dedicating all her time to looking after Elijah. He spends most of his time reading in the Vatican library. Soon he will be summoned to start his mission as world events spiral toward Iran's nuclear ambitions.

Elijah roams the Vatican halls at all hours of day and night. His mind is growing at a formidable rate. Like a sponge, it is soaking up all the knowledge he reads and learns.

One evening at dinner, Francisco decides to ask young Elijah a question. "Elijah, is the end going to be as violent as the Bible says?"

Elijah stops his fork halfway from his mouth and nods. "Yes, it will be. So many signs have been sent. It is clearly written that toward the end times, all that is happening now is preordained. All these warnings, and yet the world still does not heed them. Scientists explain them all away. People are looking for any reason to delve deeper into the sinful world Satan has created. God has given you so much, all the food to eat, from the sea and the land, all provided by God, but that was not enough. Satan has created another world that is more flavorful and more appealing to the sinners' palate. This is where so many find comfort and contentment. They all worship Satan and his corrupting ways, which will lead all who follow him into hell. Without realizing it, they are worshipping him.

"Satan's arsenal of sin is the love of money, drugs, sex, lust, power, greed, and envy. They are in high demand these days. They prove too much for unbelievers and believers to resist. So many more follow him than God. They have been perverted into thinking this is the reason why they have been brought here to Earth.

"When I am called to perform my mission, I will warn all those who are headed for the bowels of hell for eternity. Fortunately for them, our God is a forgiving God, and it is not too late. They have only to seek God's forgiveness and accept the Messiah, and they will be forgiven. That is his promise; they will be allowed to enter the kingdom of heaven."

"Will I be forgiven?" Francisco asks.

The Messenger looks deep into his eyes. "You are forgiven. Your decisions against Satan were guided by a higher power."

Francisco's posture eases, as does the tension in his face, as he lets out a long breath. "Thank you so much for that, Elijah."

Elijah shrugs. "I am just the Messenger. It is God you need to thank."

51

THE BEGINNING OF THE END

Eighteen months later, right on schedule, Iran becomes a full-blown nuclear power, having equipped itself with a nuclear arsenal as powerful as Israel's. Iran is capable of launching a massive nuclear strike against the Unites States and Israel, causing catastrophic damage.

Iran demands that Israel surrender the disputed territories and go back to its 1967 borders, but Israel refuses. Russia has aligned with Iran in the conflict, and the United States has aligned itself with Israel. It is inevitable that all four powers will be locked in a nuclear showdown. Old wounds that have never quite healed are in danger of being ripped open, triggering a true war to end all wars. Every nation is choosing sides.

The United States scrambles its forces to react to a first strike. They put their nuclear forces on DEFCON 3. Russia's forces are on high alert as well. Meanwhile, China is trying to be the voice of reason throughout the world. Has the entire world gone crazy?

The president of the United States pressures Israel to work things out with Iran. Russia does the same with Iran. Both countries know there are no winners in a nuclear war. The American president is on the phone with the Israeli prime minister, telling him Israel has the backing of the United States, but they must seek a peaceful resolution to the conflict. He insists Israel give up land for peace.

"Is the land worth ending the world for?" he asks. "If you resist, the world as you know it is over. You will have no country, nor will the United States or the rest of the world. You must do what needs to be done if the world is to survive. You have a bunch of fanatics in Iran. Negotiate with them, and end this with a peaceful solution."

The Israeli prime minister agrees and he meets with his cabinet to try to come up with a peaceful solution.

In the Vatican, Elijah meets with the Holy Father, Paul, and Francisco. "Humankind's end is near," Elijah says. "It has been revealed to me that on the sixth day of the sixth month at the sixth hour, the world will begin to destroy itself."

Despite being on Earth for only three years, Elijah has transformed into a thirty-three-year-old man, in the prime of his life. He wears his hair long and straight, draping down the sides of his face and parted in the middle. He also wears a robe reminiscent of Christ. Looking up as if talking with someone, he repeats what he is being told. "It is time to begin my mission."

He snaps out of his deep conversation with the heavens and turns to his companions. "We must travel to the Middle East. I must alert Israel and the world."

Paul, the Pope, and Francisco fall to their knees in prayer for Earth and all its inhabitants. The Pope will stay at the Vatican and alert the world's political and religious leaders of the impending crisis. He asks for prayers so that God will have mercy and spare the world from the calamity that is about to erupt.

52

REVELATION

Deep below Earth's surface, in an underground nuclear missile facility in Iran, the Beast plans the first nuclear missile attack against the United States and Israel.

In a similar facility in Israel, their nuclear defense shield is deployed, and they are calculating their response. Amazingly, they are convinced they will survive. They are calculating their loss of life and the number of injured and are trying to figure out how to minimize the nuclear fallout. They have been preparing for this day for many years and have built entire underground cities for Israel citizens so they will survive a nuclear war. Israel is in full survival mode, ready to attack and defend.

All flights in Israeli and Iranian airspace are grounded, as both sides have already accidentally shot down twelve passenger planes, mistaking them for bombers and killing thousands.

Paul, Francisco, Elijah, and Rita, who is still caring for Elijah, are flown to Jordan, where they plan to attempt to enter Israel.

With the urging of the king of Jordan, as a favor to the Pope, they are allowed into Israel. Once in the country, they press to meet with the country's leaders, but the prime minister refuses to meet with them.

In a last-ditch effort, Elijah, Paul, Francisco, and Rita stand outside the Israeli Knesset building, and Elijah begins to deliver his message to Israel. He shouts like a street preacher, burning with fire and brimstone. The Israeli Knesset members inside the building can hear Elijah's message as he yells it.

"Hear me, Israel, the end of time is upon you. Accept your Savior, the one and only true Messiah, Jesus. If you do not accept the true God, you will perish in the darkness and stench of hell and be amongst the tormenting fires. The Father loves you and has sent his only Son. He has a place in his heart for you. He will allow you to come back into the kingdom of heaven. Accept Jesus as your Savior, and you will be saved!"

All four of them are taken into custody, mostly for their own protection, as people are throwing rocks and debris at them. They are charged with disturbing government operations. In response, the Pope launches a full diplomatic protest. He asks that the prime minister see the group personally, but the prime minister is still trying to reach a diplomatic solution to his country's crisis and cannot be reached. It is an extremely demanding and tense time around the world.

The Israeli government wants Elijah and the others out of their country. "Where do you want to go?" a government representative asks them.

"We want to go to into Iran to preach God's message," Elijah replies.

They are loaded onto an unmarked plane that needs no runway. It lifts straight up like a helicopter and then, once it reaches its desired altitude, flies horizontally toward its destination.

A short time later, they set down in a desolate desert area between Iraq and Iran, where Mossad agents show them a covert way into Iran, but not before telling them not to return to Israel.

They enter Iran through a small border town that is surrounded by desert.

"Where do we go now?" Francisco asks, looking around at the desolate wilderness that surrounds them.

Elijah points toward the east. "We will go to Tehran."

They start to walk, but they are quickly surrounded by military vehicles. Due to the heightened state of alert between Israel and Iran, Iran's military intelligence observed the breach of their border through satellite images and have been closely monitoring the group's movements.

They bring the foursome to a detention center and interrogate them. Francisco is the first to be questioned. His interrogator is a portly, balding, older man in a high-ranking military uniform. They are in a small room with a desk separating them. Two Iranian men sit next to the older man, including a younger man with Iranian intelligence.

Well-built with thick black hair, the young man points an accusing finger at Francisco. "You are Mossad agents! You have come to Iran to gather information."

"I seek diplomatic immunity," Francisco replies. "I am the leader of the Jesuit Order of the Roman Catholic Church and an official member of the Holy See of Rome. We were kicked out of Israel and sent here to deliver the message from God that Israel has rejected."

"If that is true, why were you brought here by Mossad?"

Francisco leans back in his chair, unimpressed by the young man's yelling. "It was our choice to come here to give the message to your leaders."

His interrogators process his response for a moment and then get up and walk out.

Thirty minutes later, they return, armed with an abundance of pictures of Francisco and the Pope. "Superior General," the older man says in a low, non-threatening voice. "Why is the Vatican cooperating with Israeli intelligence?"

Realizing they know who he is, Francisco speaks more openly. "We are not. We were sent here on a mission to alert the world to repent before the final day is upon us."

The older man stares intently at Francisco as he takes a drag on his cigarette. "Who among you is here to deliver this message?"

Francisco's response is opaque, having vowed to protect Elijah with his dying breath. "God will let you know."

Just then, they hear someone yelling. It's Elijah. He's preaching a sermon that is coming from God. He couldn't control it if he wanted to. Like a songbird that has to sing, Elijah must preach God's message.

The two interrogators look at each other. The younger one smiles slyly. "I guess God just has."

They take Francisco back to his room and get Elijah. Rita struggles to hold onto him, but she is quickly subdued.

The men lead Elijah into the interrogation room. They sit him in the same chair as Francisco. The older man stares at Elijah, trying to gauge him. Elijah stares straight ahead, as if oblivious to all that is going on. The older man brings his cigarette to his mouth and then stops short. "Are you here to deliver a message from God?"

Elijah stares straight ahead, saying nothing. His questioner squints, insulted at being ignored. He slams his hand on the desk. "You will answer me when I speak to you! Do you understand me?"

Finally, Elijah looks at him. "May I tell you something in private?"

The man is mystified by his request. "We have no secrets here. What do you want to tell me?"

"Your son, Yusuf, told me to tell you he knows that you blame yourself for his and your wife's death. He says to tell you it was not your fault. The man driving on the other side of the highway crossed into your path. It was he who feel asleep, not you. You were knocked unconscious after the crash. It was not your fault."

The older man rises to his feet and raises his hand to hit Elijah, but then what he has heard consumes him. He walks out of the room, leaving the younger man to wonder what just happened.

After taking a few minutes to compose himself, he walks back in and asks the younger man to leave him alone with Elijah.

The older man appears humbled by his experience. "How did you know all that about me?"

"Your wife and your son are in the kingdom."

The old man lowers his head. "Are they okay?"

Elijah nods. "Your wife and son are very happy. They are together, and they want to know they love you with all their hearts. She also knows of all the new grandchildren, and she is still part of their lives as well as yours. Your last grandson will be born next year, God willing, and he will be the most like you. Your daughter will name him after Yusuf."

The man begins to cry. "Will I be with her when I die?" he asks softly, speaking through a cracking voice and watery eyes. He is a Christian man.

"Know this, Hakeem," Elijah says. "If you hear the message and receive it, you will do this before it's too late."

Hakeem nods, not at all surprised that Elijah knows his name. "I will," he says softly.

"Then you will be with her for eternity."

"Is there anything I can do for you?" Hakeem asks.

"Yes. Can you help me get a meeting with the supreme leader? I have an extremely important message for him."

Hakeem gets on the phone and calls his superior in Tehran. "We must try arranging a meeting with the supreme leader," he says. "I have interrogated the detained men with the woman, and they have a very important message for him."

The request to see the supreme leader is relayed three times to higher and higher authorities before it finally reaches the supreme leader's ears. He has his representative call Hakeem and ask what the message is.

Hakeem puts his hand over the receiver. "What is the message?"

"Heart of my heart," Elijah replies, "I will never leave you, and when I die I will send you a message from heaven. This is my promise to you."

Hakeem looks stunned, afraid to relay that message. He wonders why he didn't think to ask Elijah about the message first.

"Please, just tell him," Elijah says softly.

Hakeem cautiously relays the message, hoping a miracle can get him out of the situation. He is sure he will be shot over it.

After a tense ten-minute wait, he hears an overwhelmingly ecstatic voice pipe through the phone. "*Yella! Yella!* (Quickly! Quickly!) Yes, he will see them. Send them quickly."

53

MEETING WITH THE AYATOLLAH

Elijah, Paul, Francisco, and Rita are put on an Iranian military transport plane to Tehran. The message that Elijah sent the Ayatollah was a nursery song that the supreme leader's mother made up herself and sang often to him as a young child up until his twelfth birthday. His thoughts are often of his youth, the fond memories bringing joy to his heart.

Once they land in Tehran, they are met by a caravan of military and police vehicles and taken to the supreme leader, Ayatollah Ebrrahim Hassan.

He is waiting for them in a small mosque, a defensive tactic to throw off the Israelis, who may have a drone ready to kill him. He moves from mosque to mosque, leading his country while on a defensive trot.

They are led into the center of the mosque, which is now a makeshift international office. They are all searched for weapons and transmitting devices. When the Ayatollah receives the all-clear signal, he makes his way into the mosque through the back door.

He is accompanied by his inner circle of elite religious scholars, all dressed in robes and turbans and wearing full beards. Also with him are the most seasoned military and intelligence minds in the country. Most are in military uniforms, except for the intelligence officers, who are dressed in suits and street clothes. They are all either clean shaven or have mustaches. They advise and update the Ayatollah constantly on the current crisis.

The four visitors stand abreast in front of him. The Ayatollah looks at Paul and sees blood soaking through the bandages on his wrists. He asks for the bandages to be removed and sees the wounds of Christ on Paul. Feeling skeptical, he looks at Rita, whose eyes are fixed on Francisco, whom the Ayatollah senses is a member of the clergy. When he looks at Elijah, he gets a completely different feeling, holy in nature.

He calls his team of trusted religious advisers into a huddle. A moment later, they ask Elijah to step forward. The advisors assemble behind the Ayatollah as he examines the young man. "Was it you who sent me the message?"

Elijah nods. "Yes."

"What is your name?"

"Elijah."

The Ayatollah looks at his staff and nods at a man who is a Bible scholar, Iran's ambassador to the Holy See. The man has a grayish beard and wears a white turban and a dark robe. He steps into the huddle and converses with the Ayatollah.

"Who is Elijah in their scripture?" the Ayatollah asks.

"He is supposed to appear on Earth in its last days," his Vatican ambassador says. "He is the messenger who will alert the world of the Second Coming of their Messiah, Christ. He is a modern-day version of John the Baptist, who told of their Messiah's first coming. In the Second Coming, Christ will come down from heaven riding on the clouds with an army of angels and Michael, the Archangel. They will battle Satan and his forces, crush the devil, and send him to hell for eternity."

Nodding sagely as he digests all he has heard, the Ayatollah turns to Elijah. "Walk with me." He motions for Elijah to accompany him outside into a garden, which is covered with thick brush so the Ayatollah cannot be seen by any satellite, thus preventing him from being hit by a drone strike. The garden is also a private place out of earshot of everyone else.

The two men sit down at a table in the middle of the garden, where refreshments are served. They talk for an hour before ending their meeting. No one else is allowed to hear their words.

Afterwards, the Ayatollah orders Paul and the others to be taken to the Roman Catholic Church of the Consolata, also known as the Roman Catholic Cathedral of Tehran, where they can live with the Catholic community. They will stay in Tehran as guests of the Iranian government. The Christian Assyrian population has populated that area of Tehran with a smaller Roman Catholic presence. These are the Assyrians who left Iraq in the post-Saddam Hussein era due to massive abuses perpetrated against Iraq's Christian population.

The Ayatollah returns to his underground nuclear missile facility, where Iran will order missile strikes against the United States and Israel. The command center is well below the earth's surface, built to withstand a bunker-buster bomb.

Gilani, the young and charismatic president of Iran, along with the highest-ranking generals in charge of Iran's nuclear missile program on land and sea, is mapping out the missile attacks to inflict maximum damage. Iran has nuclear submarines hiding in the Straits of Hormuz, which are able to hit Israel from the sea with extreme accuracy. Gilani is ratcheting up the rhetoric in his talks to the Israeli prime minister from the control room via video conferencing.

The huge TV screen lights up, and the Israeli prime minster appears. "Prime Minister Gilani, Israel is still committed to ending this conflict with a peaceful resolution. Nikita Khrushchev, the leader of Russia, once told John Kennedy, a young president like you, 'Do not tie a knot so tight that it cannot be untied.' We seek peace, not war. We do not want to end the world."

Gilani looks at the screen in disdain. "You Zionists are only interested in one thing: owning and controlling the world. You merely disguise your intentions of world domination. If you are serious, leave the occupied territories."

"I will say this to you again: We are open to discussions."

"We have been having discussions with you!" Ali yells. "For fifty years! And you only expand your borders while we talk. You keep taking land that doesn't belong to you. If you want to stop this war and your annihilation, pull your expansionist movement back to your original borders."

The prime minister looks back at his advisors in bewilderment and then turns back to the camera. "We will start to pull back from some of the disputed areas, in the interest of peace, and to end the possibility of a world calamity, which this conflict will cause. We make this offering to you for the sake of peace. We will withdraw ten thousand settlers from the disputed territories."

In truth, Gilani does not want to stop the imminent destruction. Instead, he wants the conflict to accelerate. "No, all the territories, and you will go back to your 1967 borders. Then only can there be peace in the region." He knows Israel will not accept that, so he can keep the fire of destruction alive.

"Give me time, and I will get back to you," the prime minister says.

As soon as the screen goes black, Israel goes into full attack mode, their missile defense systems on high alert.

54

CLOUDS OF DOOM

Israeli attack jets report the phenomenon, as do Iranian fighter pilots. Staring at the clouds, Elijah speaks outside of St. Mary's Park in Tehran, standing on a bench next to a statue of the Blessed Mother and her child, Jesus. "Look above at the clouds! They are transporting God's angelic warriors. They are upon us! Repent! The time is getting near and shorter. Hear me: Accept the Lord Jesus, as your Savior! There will be rattling of teeth and fear of the creatures that will inhabit Earth. Quickly, save your soul! The anointed one's time is near; his coming is at hand. Hear me, oh Israel! Save yourself. He has given you a second chance to accept the true and only God, the Lord and Savior, Jesus Christ." Elijah's voice cracks with emotion as he preaches. "He loves you and wants you to come into the fold of his heavenly kingdom."

All Israel hears his voice. Search parties are sent out looking for him within Israel so they can stop his preaching, to no avail.

The Christian world is in deep prayer, asking for God to save them and spare them from the apocalypse. Billions of prayers are offered up.

The monitor in Iran's nuclear bunker rings again. It's the Israeli prime minster. "In the interest of peace, we will withdraw twenty thousand settlers from the disputed territories and concede that land to you. We are also open to further negotiations."

The Ayatollah sees it as a victory for Iran. From his perspective, the crisis is over, and his side has won.

Gilani, the Beast, sees things differently. He shoots down the gesture of peace as too little too late. He replies without consulting with the Ayatollah or the Supreme Council. "All or nothing," he says, itching to provoke Israel into a nuclear war.

The Ayatollah asks Gilani to come to his quarters at the nuclear facility. When Gilani enters, he bows to the Ayatollah and places his hand over his heart.

The Ayatollah does not even ask him to sit down. "Ali, why did you not consult with me or anyone from the Supreme Council before you rejected the Israeli's offer?"

Gilani looks stunned that he is being questioned about his decision, thinking he had everyone on the Supreme Council under his spell. "It was not good for Iran or the region. Surely you would have rejected that offer?"

The Ayatollah stands up. "You will never know, because you never bothered to ask."

Gilani pretends to humble himself before the Ayatollah. "Supreme Leader, it is only in your interest that I make such a decision. We would not want the world to believe that Iran has backed down from Israel."

The Ayatollah looks at him with disgust, knowing he is being conned. Then he smiles and looks away. "Oh, yes, after thinking about it, I realize you did have my best interest in mind. I support you in your decision. Please do not let me detain you from your posts at the control room. You are needed there."

As soon as Gilani is gone, the Ayatollah calls for a private meeting with the Supreme Council. He also calls his religious scholar and closest advisor to the meeting. They gather in a private conference room in the massive underground faculty. A surprise guest also appears at the meeting: Elijah.

After the meeting, the leaders of the Supreme Council gather in the control room. Gilani greets them with a traditional bow and puts his hand over his heart, but the council does not reply in kind. He begins to update them on Israel's aggressive posture and recommends launching missiles at Israel and the United States immediately.

"Do you want to end the world, President Gilani?" the Ayatollah asks.

"I am only doing your and the Supreme Council's will," Gilani replies. "We cannot wait. We must launch now, before Israel and the United States launch a first strike against us."

"You made this decision without considering anyone else's point of view," the Ayatollah says.

"This is beyond all of you," Gilani says, sneering. He looks at the general. "Launch the missiles!"

When the general doesn't move, he pushes the general aside and then enters the launch codes himself. The council looks at him with pure hatred. Little does he realize the Ayatollah has changed the launch codes.

When none of the missiles launch, Gilani looks stunned. He knows he's been outsmarted by the Ayatollah. Realizing he has only one card left to play, he calls out for help from the one who spawned him. "Father, finish what we have started."

The Supreme Council surrounds the Beast and pulls long, thin knives from under their robes as the Ayatollah steps back.

As the council members stab Gilani, he feels the steel blades enter his stomach, bladder, and spine. "Father, help me!" he screams. He staggers into a member of the Supreme Council, who stabs him again and spits on him.

"You are nothing compared to Satan!" Gilani yells as he clutches his wounds.

"Where is your Satan now?" one of the council members asks.

As he is spit upon and stabbed, Gilani's screams start to resemble that of a wild swine.

Throughout it all, somehow he musters the strength and the ability to override the panel's safeguard and, with Satan's help, launch one missile.

"Thank you, Father," he says as his body degenerates, taking on the appearance of a demon.

He begins to crawl, but the council members kick and stab him repeatedly until he falls over, dead.

Some soldiers enter and drag away his body.

The monitor goes on again. It is the president of the United States. "Where is your president?" he asks, seeing only the Ayatollah and the religious leaders around the room.

"I am in charge from now on," the Ayatollah says. "You will be speaking to me."

"Did you fire that missile intentionally?" the president asks.

"No, it was an accident."

The president turns and orders the missile to be destroyed when it reaches Earth's outer atmosphere. All the major nuclear powers are listening in, preparing to unleash their arsenals, but they wait to see the American president's next move. He has heard everything that's happened in the Iranian faculty, thanks to listening devices planted there by the National Security Agency. If it were a true strike, it would have been met with a full response, setting off every other nuclear power. The president is already in the air, onboard Air Force One, the presidential jet. This will ensure his safety and the safety of his family and his key cabinet members.

"The people of the United States seek peace; will you join us?"

"If you are truthful and sincere in your proposals, then, yes, Iran will join you," the Ayatollah says.

"I must tell you, that missile you launched, whether intentionally or not, if we are unable to neutralize it, and it hits the United States, we will have no choice but to retaliate. We will take out one of your major cities in an equally damaging attack on your country. Pray we are able to intercept it outside Earth's atmosphere."

55

ON THE RAZOR'S EDGE

The large clouds over the Middle East start to take on a more aggressive and menacing posture. Two Israeli fighter jets are ordered to take a closer look.

As the jets approach the clouds, the pilots see what appears to be an army of human figures. They are on the clouds and dressed in ancient military armor with swords in their hands. Leading them all is the Archangel Michael. He motions with his sword for the fighter jets to leave.

The pilots stare in disbelief, thinking it's a diversion or trick by the Iranians. They set their course to fly straight through the clouds.

As they approach, Michael dips his sword in a defensive maneuver that causes a huge flash of electricity. A bolt of lightning deflects off his sword and hits the jets. They spin away, but then the autopilot takes over, correcting their course. The pilots are unharmed. It was only a warning. Both jets are ordered back to their base in Israel.

When the pilots try to explain what happened, no one believes them, and an Israeli Air Force general decides to fly up there to get a firsthand look.

He is loaded with destructive missiles. He reaches the clouds and sees the same thing as the fighter pilots before him. He takes aim, locks in on his targets, and presses the "launch" button. Nothing happens. Then he attempts the same maneuver as the previous pilots, to fly through the clouds. The Archangel Michael waves him off just like he did the others.

Determined, the general circles back and heads for the cloud formation. Michael dips his sword, unleashing a blast of lightning. It hits the plane and takes over its controls, guiding the plane over the water and releasing its missiles into the sea. Then it lands the plane safely back at its base. The Israeli general is converted to Christianity right there on the tarmac.

The president of the United States watches as America's defensive missiles head for the Iranian missile, which is just outside the atmosphere. The first one misses wildly, but the second one seems to be right on course.

All feel relieved, until the defensive missile explodes before it hits its target. The nuclear missile continues toward the United States, on course to hit Washington, DC.

The president remembers an admiral in charge of the USS *Lake Erie*, a nuclear submarine that was able to shoot down a useless satellite outside of Earth's atmosphere before it could reenter and cause harm. Some believe it was to show China that their successful attempt to take out one of their old satellites was primitive by comparison.

The president orders the USS *Lake Erie* to intercept the rogue missile. It turns out the submarine is in the exact position required to do the job—off the coast of Iran in the Persian Gulf.

The submarine's missile blasts up from the Persian Gulf, scaring all aboard a small Iranian navy frigate. They had no idea they were sitting right on top of a US submarine. As the missile illuminates the night sky, it looks like it's starting to fall backwards into the sea. Just then, the next stage of the missile ignites, and it blasts off into space.

Traveling some seventeen thousand miles per hour, it veers off course slightly, preventing it from intercepting the rogue missile. A kinetic kill switch attached to the missile is turned on. Now it can see the target and change its course, heading for a direct intercept. The rogue missile starts to enter Earth's atmosphere.

Just as it reaches the point of no return, the US missile slams into the Iranian missile, causing a powerful explosion. The target is destroyed.

The National Military Command Center at the Pentagon is ecstatic. They share tears and cheers with each other as well as their counterparts in Russia, China, Israel, Iran, and every other country. The world sighs with relief that they will be allowed to live another day, by the grace of God.

The large clouds over the Middle East start to break apart, and then they shoot into the heavens.

The crisis avoided, Elijah looks at Paul, Francisco, and his mother, Rita. "It's over."

"What are you going to do now?" Francisco asks.

"This is just a delay," Elijah says. "The Father has answered so many prayers for those who need more time. My mission is still ongoing. This conflict will reignite, and the world will destroy itself. But for now, I will spread the message of the Second Coming, for it will soon be at hand."

56

NEVER ADD INSULT TO INJURY

Eager to recruit Johnny into his crew to succeed him as the boss, Tomas sends for him one last time, using one of his most trusted men. Johnny knows what Tomas wants, so he has been avoiding him and ignoring his previous requests, enraging the old man.

Johnny is shopping in the Arthur Avenue market, an indoor marketplace that is a world unto itself, a relic of a bygone era. Fruit stands and butcher shops stand alongside quaint shops in what feels like an open-air market but is shielded from the elements in a controlled environment. The marketplace was established when Italian immigrants came to New York by the hundreds of thousands. It is a scene frozen in time that still exists today.

Johnny approaches Joe, the owner of a deli. "Can you make me a fresh mozzarella, tomato, and prosciutto sandwich?"

"Sure, Johnny," Joe replies.

As Johnny waits, he receives a tap on his shoulder. He turns around to see a man with a full head of hair and a round face with a slightly pronounced nose that fits onto his still handsome and charismatic face. It takes Johnny a minute, but he knows the face. Then it dawns on him; it's Louie "Squash" Spaziro.

"Hey, Johnny, how are you doing?" Louie says.

Johnny has not seen Squash in many years and is overjoyed to see his boyhood friend. They reminisce and laugh about their childhood days.

Once they're all caught up, Louie turns serious and places his hand on Johnny's shoulder. "The old man has been looking for you for a long time. You really need to go see him. He's at his restaurant. Do us all a favor and go now, before things get messy."

Johnny nods. "Okay."

Louie gives Johnny's shoulder a squeeze and then walks off.

Johnny knows what Tomas wants, but he is beginning to be changed by something he does not understand. His mind craves something different. It's a hunger he cannot ignore, intensifying with every moment, and a constant and undeniable pulling of his thoughts. They are constantly on Francisco and his men.

Johnny leaves the market, but instead of going to Tomas, he goes to see Monsignor Mariano at Mount Carmel Church.

After this latest snub, Tomas is no longer seeking Johnny to join him but to eliminate him. He is a true gangster who feels he has been disrespected and taken advantage of. Now he must exact his revenge. A hit is an unwanted nuisance, but it is a necessary evil to maintain order in his world.

He summons his most experienced and dangerous assassins, experts in deception and death. They are not at all like Rashid or Large Louis. They are patient, elite killers. They have fallen off the radar of law enforcement and are only called upon when their skills are truly needed. They leave no traces. It's as if the service they provide is done by the wind or comes out of the air itself. For Johnny to try to fight them off would be futile. Their numbers and their skill are too great.

The next afternoon, Tomas walks across the street from his restaurant to a small gated park, where a large bust of Christopher Columbus stands proudly. It represents the Italian-American population of Arthur Avenue. An older man, Anthony Brooklyn, enters the park with a walker. He is wearing a white collared shirt with short sleeves, wire-rimmed glasses, dress pants, and sneakers. His teeth are discolored due to excessive age. He looks like a great-grandfather near the end of his life.

Accompanying Anthony Brooklyn are what appear to be two caretakers. They are young, handsome, well-built, dark-skinned Italian men with jet-black hair. The taller of the two, Franco, wears sunglasses as he stands beside Frankie, a.k.a. "Nuts and Bolts." He has been shot so many times that his bones and skull have so much metal plating and steel rods inserted in them that he sets off metal detectors wherever he goes. His shootouts with law enforcement and street gangs are legendary. Both are in their early thirties. They help the old man as he sits at a checker table made of concrete. Tomas arrives and sits on the other side of the table.

"Hello, Tomas," the old man says.

"I'd give you a kiss," Tomas replies, "but if the feds are watching us, it would be a sign to them."

Anthony Brooklyn chuckles. "I did not come all the way out here from Brooklyn to be kissed by you."

Tomas returns the comic slight with a chuckle of his own. Then they get down to the business of plotting to kill. The two younger men posing as aides will most likely be called to do the hit. They are young and eager, wanting to gain position and power in the organization.

"Tomas, you've never called for our services before," the old man rasps. "Someone must have really gotten on your bad side."

"Oh, that he did," Tomas replies, nodding slowly.

The old man studies Tomas's angry face. "Who is he?"

Tomas grunts. "Johnny Ciminetti."

The younger men know Johnny well, having served time with him in prison.

Great, Franco thinks. *A well-known guy. This hit will make me move up quickly in the ranks.* He is intrigued and hot to do it as Tomas and the old man go over Johnny's history, his habits, and everything needed to complete a successful hit.

The old man will find the best way to perform the murder so it will be undetectable. The hit is on, and the assassins are dispatched.

57

THE UNLUCKY, LUCKY ONE

Johnny has been staying at the church and the rectory for the last two weeks and has not left. The monsignor has talked with Johnny and has contacted Francisco, who is back in Rome. Francisco has spoken with Johnny and asked him many questions about what he is feeling of late. He has determined that Johnny has received a true calling from God. He knows the feeling well. Francisco informs the monsignor that he will be returning to Mount Carmel.

Oh no, not again! the monsignor thinks in despair.

Late one night at his restaurant, Tomas is sitting at a table, about to close, when he looks out the window and sees a limousine pull up in front. He is elated to see the Archbishop of New York, Cardinal Terrance O'Hare, get out. Then the driver opens the other rear door, and Francisco gets out. Tomas thinks they are probably going to another restaurant, but then they walk toward his front door, accompanied by two of Francisco's men. Francisco is carrying a large red-and-white paisley satchel.

They walk into the restaurant and are greeted by the maître d', who bends to kiss the cardinal's ring. "Cardinal O'Hare, please come in. Sit anywhere you like."

"Thank you," the cardinal replies, smiling. They sit in the back, where Tomas is sitting. Francisco's men sit two tables away from the cardinal and Francisco, though still close by.

"Would you care to join us, Tomas?" the cardinal asks.

Tomas gives the cardinal an odd look, wondering how he knows his name. Then he straightens himself upright. "Yes, I would like that very much," he replies. Tommaso feels he is a good Catholic despite all his illegal activities.

Tomas joins Francisco and the cardinal. He orders several different dishes and wines for them to taste.

"I have a gift from the Holy Father for you," Francisco says. He pushes the large satchel toward Tomas. It is filled with expensive artifacts with stones of many different colors and sizes, large pieces of gold, and large diamonds.

Tomas stares at its contents in disbelief and then looks up at Francisco. "I appreciate your gifts, but how does the Pope know me? For that matter, how do you, Cardinal O'Hare?"

Cardinal O'Hare excuses himself from the table, leaving Francisco alone with Tomas. "We know you because of Johnny Ciminetti," Francisco says.

Tomas reels in shock. "Oh, so you're the priest from Rome. Can you tell me where Ciminetti is?" he asks slyly.

"I can't tell you that, but I can tell you that he has changed his life."

"What, has Ciminetti become religious, because he's had a couple of confessions?"

Francisco smiles and shakes his head. "No, I'm happy to say much more than that. We want to thank you for helping us. Please accept this gift for your help and to cease in any aggression toward Johnny or his family."

"That is one unappreciative bastard," Tomas says.

Francisco frowns at Tomas's reaction. "What I have brought you here in the way of a gift is worth at least one thousand times more than whatever you have given or invested in him, and that's a very conservative estimate."

Tomas sighs. "It's not about that."

"Are you having trouble letting this go?"

"Actually, I am, yes."

Francisco would rather not have to give Tomas this message, but he has no other choice. "The Holy Father has instructed me to tell you if you cannot see it in your heart to let it go, all the Church's resources will be used to stop any aggression toward Johnny and his family."

Stunned, Tomas knows exactly what that means. The political power of the Church still wields great influence and will cause a lot of exposure and scrutiny from the public, politicians, and law enforcement. It could lead to a lot of trouble for him and his organization.

Tomas looks at the floor in disgust, realizing the wise old Jesuit has him in checkmate. Finally, he relents. "Okay, I'll leave it alone," he says. The satchel has softened the blow quite a bit.

He summons Louie from the bar. "Call Brooklyn," Tomas whispers in his ear. "Tell them it's off. And do it right away." Just like that, it's over.

The two weeks that Johnny has been at the church receiving his calling has saved his life. His assassins were perched at all the places he normally frequented, ready to bring about his demise. Luckily for Johnny, Mount Carmel Church was not one of those places.

Francisco thanks Tomas for dealing with things amicably.

Tomas points at the satchel. "Really, I don't need that, but I'll take it anyway, only because it's a gift from the Pope and from you." Tomas smiles brightly, pulling the satchel closer to him.

Francisco grins at Tomas's attempt to hide his extreme desire for the gift. Then the cardinal rejoins the men, and they trade stories as they enjoy their dining experience.

58

THE LORD WORKS IN STRANGE WAYS

The phone rings back at the Ciminettis' house in the Bronx. Philomena picks up the antiquated receiver. "Hello?"

A pleasing, familiar voice is on the other end of the line: Joel Rosenbaum. "Hello, Philomena, I'm back in New York. I just wanted to tell you I will be on time tonight for your kosher Italian."

She smiles in excitement. "It will be ready. Johnny will be here, as will Reggie and Lena. They'll all be so happy to see you."

"Yes, it will be great to see you all again," Joel replies. "Seven o' clock, yes?"

Philomena stirs a pot as she answers. "Yes, perfect."

Philomena's doorbell rings at precisely seven o' clock. "It smells great in here, as usual," Joel says when she opens the door.

Little Philomena runs and jumps into her mother's arms. Lena gives Philomena a kiss on her cheek. "Bye, Grandma. I'm off to a modeling shoot in the city. Please don't wait up again tonight. It may take all night. I love you." Philomena has taken Lena in as her own, a sister to Reggie, who is back in school and finishing college, enjoying a normal life with her family.

Joel looks around. "Where's Johnny?"

Philomena smiles. "He'll be right down."

Joel hears the steps creak and looks up to see Johnny wearing a long black Jesuit priest's outfit, adorned with the traditional thirty-three buttons to honor the life of Christ and the traditional priestly white color. Joel's eyes widen in shock. "What? Where, when, how did this happen?"

Johnny puts his arm around Joel and smiles. "You seem surprised. A miraculous and stunning calling from God has entered me. I am with

God, and he is with me."

Joel looks at Philomena, who has tears in her eyes. "I am so happy now," she says. "God has brought us all together, and my life and the lives of my family have been saved."

Shaking off her emotions, she wipes the tears of joy from her cheeks. "Time to sit down now," she says hurriedly. "*Mangia.*"

ACKNOWLEDGMENTS

To Saint Padre Pio of Pietrelcina, Italy, one of the inspirations for my book.
To my fifth-grade teacher, Miss Paula McCrudden, who first inspired me
to write.
To my mother, who left life too early.
To Dad, who loved all his children.
To my brothers and sisters, without whom I would not be here.
To my brother-in-law, Mike, who has been a constant foundation
throughout the years.
To my daughter, Jennifer, who has spent countless hours helping me.
To Monique Disalvo for her help with social media for this book.
And truly, there are so many others.
Thank you.

ABOUT THE AUTHOR

Antonio Martello grew up in the Arthur Avenue/Belmont/Fordham section of the Bronx, New York, right across the street from the Bronx Zoo. His upbringing inspired many of the characters in his book. It was a different time when respect meant much more than it does today.

Antonio went through the local public schools system, and Public School 32 is where he first received strong encouragement and support in writing, from his fifth-grade teacher, Paula McCrudden. She assigned the class to write a mystery story. She liked Antonio's story so much she entered it in a contest, and it won. It was featured and published in a college newspaper. That assignment and its effects still resonate with Antonio today. Miss McCrudden's belief in him will never be forgotten and is one of his major reasons for writing.

Switching from public school to Saint Helena's High School, a Catholic high school in the Bronx, was equally inspiring. Antonio's classes with his history teacher, Mr. Stork, regarding current events and world history piqued Antonio's interests and made those subjects his life's passion, a passion that is reflected in his writing today.

CPSIA information can be obtained
at www.ICGtesting.com
Printed in the USA
LVHW081957310719
626017LV00010B/170/P